DEADLY SINS
A POLITICAL ANTHOLOGY

By
TL James
C. Highsmith-Hooks
Lorita Kelsey Childress
Jazz Singleton
Linda Watson
Michele T. Darring
Jean Holloway

Published by PHE Ink – Writing Solutions Firm
9597 Jones Rd #213
Houston, TX 77065

PHE Ink and the portrayal of the quill feather are
trademarks of PHE Ink.

The cataloging-in-publication data is on file with the
Library of Congress.

Library of Congress Control Number: 2001012345

ISBN: Print - 978-1-935724-10-0
ISBN: eBook - 978-1-935724-61-2

Printed in the United States of America

February 2013
Genre: Political Anthology

Editing by Jean Holloway
Cover Design by TL James

TABLE OF CONTENTS

DAY ONE

SEVEN DAYS ··· SEVEN SINS

Matthew tapped his fingers in a rhythmic motion as he watched the polls for the upcoming 2012 election. With each uptick in the opponent's ratings, Matthew stomach soured more. He started thinking back to the last election. Heaven had been victorious that time. Although it presented a non-bias stance, its influence proved powerful and the rightful 44th president was elected. It was very important for humanity at large, not just the United States, for President 44 to be in office. Heaven and its influential party were ready to change the world and send a global message that Humanity Cares and Saves. However, it turned bad when Heaven switched its focus onto Matthew. As he wandered further into the world, he was getting beyond the angels' reach. It was to the point that God would have been the only one to save him. Heaven pulled together to get Matthew back to Heaven, alive and in one piece. It was good for humanity that The General of Heaven's Army was home. However, it left President 44 to fend for himself against the political wolves.

Unfortunately, Matthew didn't want to be saved nor did he want Heaven's attention on him. Heaven worked really hard to beg, persuade and even threatened him to get him back to his rightful position. But he didn't care. He wanted to be with his greatest love – Mallory Haulm. Everything was going fine until Mallory learned of his true identity. Mallory was Death, the Final Fourth Horseman. He was the one that Matthew was supposed to battle in the event Armageddon should start this century. They were lovers and didn't mind the truth until his family got in the way and skewered Mallory's thinking. Then when Hell got involved, his life plans changed. Unfortunately, Mallory's plans didn't include Matthew anymore. Finally, all hell broke loose and Mallory was killed.

2

His greatest love was dead and Matthew was heartbroken. He wandered around until he found himself in the arms of none other than – Silas Xavier Luxapher or Satan, the ruler of Hell for the 21st century. That was a new low, but it didn't motivate Matthew back to Heaven. In fact, he started to get comfortable when he made himself at home at Silas residence. Silas vehemently obliged. To make matters worse, he thought he rekindled with his greatest love's soul in a series of female bodies. However, that left a series of murdered bodies. Matthew was digging himself further into a hole that was getting beyond Heaven's reach.

In a twist of fate, Heaven received a miracle. Matthew encountered a young petite red-haired woman by the name of MadySin Quinn. In route to find her family's identity, MadySin needed to retrieve an artifact from Silas' home. When Matthew stopped her from leaving, she killed him by stabbing him in the neck with her four-inch stiletto. (But that's another story)

The guilt began choking Matthew, so he tried to stop reliving the past. He was in Heaven now and he needed to get things back on track. He needed to prove to Heaven and himself that he was The Second Coming, General of Heaven's Army and the strong hand of God.

Matthew picked up the remote and quickly flipped through the channels. More politicians were beginning to speak honestly about their views. This would have been a good thing; however their views were skewed and detrimental to the majority.

"Marriage is between a man and a woman. It's a sin against God for homosexual to marry." The congressman proclaimed.

"It's also a sin for you to cheat on your wife and covet your brother's fortunes, but you're talking." Matthew answered back to the television while the man went on to explain. He dropped his head in his hands and asked, "What if you're an angel in love with a man?"

As the congressman began to degrade people for their choices, Matthew's mind floated back to his greatest love – Mallory. He loved him with every moral and immoral fiber of his being. He left Heaven for that reason – to be with Mallory. His attention snapped back to the television when he heard the congressman say, "In a legitimate rape...the body has a way to shut that stuff down."

"Legitimate rape?" He screamed out. "Oh, it's getting bad quickly." He stood up and gathered his papers in a pile and searched for a folder. He stopped in his tracks. "How are you gonna to fix this, Matty?"

He thought about it. *How was he going to fix this?* He had no ideas, had lost his influential contacts and his reputation was bruised. He slouched down in his seat in defeat. "You're useless... why did you even come back?" Matthew started berating himself for every decision, every mistake, even down to his very existence. He got up and walked over the mirror and scolded himself more. "USELESS MASS OF NOTHING! You can't even come up with a good idea. You have no influential power...NOBODY LIKES YOU!" He huffed, "If you were Silas," he paused. If he *was* Silas...If he was Silas, he would get his minions to manipulate the system for him. Matthew sat back down and looked over his notes again. Most of these people were Silas' clients. "It's a sin to lust over someone's power, but is it a sin to manipulate?" He gathered his papers and shoved them in the folder, stood up and walked over to the mirror again. "I might not have minions or influential powerful anymore, but I can manipulate one. Now all I have to do is summon him." The sour stomach returned, but with a vengeance of fear. "You weak ass...Bite the bullet, Matthew and summon him NOW!"

Silas was six bodies deep in a mosh pit of men. He entwined himself between two guys, while the one found himself at the head of the bed. "Hey...I thought we came over here for dominoes?" The guy laughed while Silas stroked him.

"Don't you like the bone you playing with?" Silas growled.

In that moment, a ray of light grew from out of the corner and practically blinded the men in the bed. Silas was too busy pleasuring himself to notice the room getting brighter. It wasn't until the men stop responding to his touches that he looked up and saw the angel standing in the room.

"DAMN IT! What is it now? God got lost in Portsborough, New York again? TWO WORDS... GPS, BITCH!"

"Sir, you have been summoned to Heaven." The angel responded as it floated toward the bed.

"WHY? Can't you see that I'm busy?"

"Sir, this is urgent."

"EVERYTHING IS URGENT IN HEAVEN!" Silas went back to nibbling on the man's neck.

"SIR!" The angel touched his shoulder and sent an electric shock through his body.

"SIR, NOTHING!" Silas managed to crawl out of the bed and began cornering the angel. "Maybe I should work you over before I go to Heaven. Lay you out on the bed, spread eagle, clip these virgin wings and wear yo' ass out—"Before he could fix his statement, the angel disappeared which infuriated Silas. He started banging his head against the wall.

"Are you in trouble?"

4

"No! When I'm in trouble they bring four angels. Two if I'm summoned by God." Silas finished his thought internally, *this time it was one angel. Something's not right.*

"Are you going up there now?"

"Yeah!" Silas rushed to the closet. "The quicker I get there, the quicker I get back."

Matthew walked around for what seemed like an eternity until he reached the edge of Heaven. As the billowy clouds turned into grassy patches, he finally found a remote place away from the pearly gates. It was very hard to find a secluded place around Heaven, but the conversation he was going to have needed to stay very private. He changed locations three times before deciding on a rock overlooking a brook that led down to Earth. As he settled in, he noticed the clouds changing with lightning flashes across the sky.

5

"Silas is right on time," Matthew mumbled as he tried to convince himself that he should not be nervous. Why was he nervous? Was it because he needed to convince the greatest con-artist alive to deliver an election or was it because he was coming face-to-face with a man who knew all his intimate thoughts. Whatever it was, if this was going to work Matthew needed to shake the feelings off. After a while, he heard bickering in the distance. Climbing up a hill, a tall, muscular man dressed in all white appeared. Matthew grabbed his knee to stop it from shaking.

"YOU KNOW GOOD AND GOT DAMN WELL I DON'T LIKE BEING SUMMONED UP HERE! NO! I DIDN'T DO IT! NO! I DON'T KNOW WHY—"

"Shut up, Satan. You're not in trouble...this time." Matthew tried to mask his nervousness with a power stance.

"EXCUSE YOU! You need to refer to me by my Christian name. Try again!" Silas hated being called Satan or being reminded that he was the one true evil. Matthew smiled and raised his hands in defeat. "So, if I'm not in trouble, why are you here then?"

"'Cause we have intimate history and I was thinking that we could—"

"Liar!" Silas stomped up to him and forcefully planted his foot on the rock between Matthew's legs. "What do you want, General's Army?"

"No hello?"

"HELL NO!" Silas angrily shouted, but he couldn't hold his anger for long. They did have an intimate history. He finally broke a smile when he saw Matthew get up for a hug. "How yah doin'? How yah mamma doin'? How yah Daddy doin'?"

He bear-hugged Silas tight, then quickly retreated when he remembered how good Silas felt. "Fine! Dad sends His regards." Matthew quickly sat back down.

6

Silas lingered for a bit before stepping back. "So I see that you made it back to Heaven, huh? We miss you on Earth, just kidding!" Silas placed his foot between Matthew's legs again. This time it pissed Matthew off.

"Yeah, but I'm on administrative restriction until they determine my loyalty...something about not slipping." Matthew pushed his foot of the rock.

"Don't worry about it. There can only be one Second Coming. You're it, babe...until then we will wait. I always say don't rush Death and the Reckoning. SO TAKE YO TIME! You got my support to take it slow." Silas leaned over and sincerely patted Matthew on the back. "Now that we're done with the small talk, why am I here?" Silas wiped his hands up and down on his shoulders and pants as if wiping dirt off of his body. Silas was glad that the moment was over. A second longer, he would have regretted Matthew being back in Heaven. He didn't want to rekindle that flame. That flame needed to stay dead and cold.

Matthew finally put on his game face. He pulled a folder from under his jacket and handed it to Silas.

"I don't want that!" Silas stepped back and pushed the folder away.

"Take the folder, you dumb ass." Matthew shoved it back to him. "I need you to look at this. It's election time again."

"Didn't we just have an election last week?"

"It does seem like it was last week...but in actuality four years have passed. That last election with the Rogue Bimbo and the Old Vet was easy. With our combine coalition between Heaven and Hell, everything went smoothly with minimum interference. But this year is different. The tactics they are using are vicious and violent. It's detrimental to humanity. It requires a lot of work that we can't deliver this time." Matthew looked away and lowered his voice. "So...He wants to outsource this completely to you."

"Easy, he says...smooth, he says...minimum interference, he says...okay." Silas flipped through the folder until he caught the last of Matthew's comment. "OUTSOURCE? WHAT DA F—"

7

"SILAS! We're in Heaven...you know better."

"I know that this is a trap. Outsource...what the hell does He mean, outsource?"

"This election is harder...dirtier. At least with the Rogue Bimbo and the Old Vet, they believed in God...and they were God fearing. This candidate and henchmen are sinister, the Devil incarnate."

"NO, THEY AIN'T! I give out that title...and there has only been ONE to hold it." Silas tried to give Matthew an evil smirk, but he quickly looked away. Matthew knew that Silas was referring to their shared love – the reason why Matthew left Heaven in the first place - Mallory Haulm. "Anyway, so the Ole Man don't want to get His hands dirty on this."

"He called in a lot of favors for the last election, but President 44 hasn't had much time to make good on his promises...given the inherited situation. So...we can't call on those people yet. Besides, we need a lot more favors for this election."

As he flipped through the files, Silas saw the Super Pacs, media outlets, and political associations that were not only stockpiling money toward this campaign, but even printing fake money to throw at it. Furthermore, he saw companies that were building unholy alliance with these groups. On any other day, this would have made Silas proud; but he was called on by the Higher Power. Silas was too busy studying the files to listen Matthew explaining the difficulties of the elections. It was only after Matthew was silent for a while that Silas looked up. "Why'd you stopped talking? I heard you. Then call in more favors."

Matthew didn't want to explain why Heaven couldn't call in favors or interfere in this election. "We don't want to take that route." Matthew cleared his throat, looked Silas dead in the eyes and lied, "He wants you to handle it alone."

"ALONE?" He closed the folder. "Define alone."

8

"He wants you to manage this election alone. You call ALL the shots to ensure that President 44 wins again...he needs to fulfill his promises. Humanity depends on it. If Heaven gets involved this time...it will look fixed. So He thought that you can use whatever you need to deliver the election... anything you need...but you only have seven days to deliver...starting today."

"That's sounds like free reign. What's the catch?"

"There's no catch. You have complete control of this..." Matthew thought he saw pride glow across Silas' face.

"No interference from anyone...not even the four Hench-horsemen?"

"NOPE! Long live The MPire. No interference from them. Besides, they are on another assignment and they don't get involved in the political arena." Matthew paused, then proclaimed. "He said, and I quote...DO YOU!"

Seven days...seven sins...the race to the White House...who will win? Silas sang to the verse in his mind several times. He looked at Matthew and then down at the files again. "Do me, huh?" he mumbled. "Well, most of these people are my constituents and some are my direct clients...And they did choose this candidate behind my back..." Silas quickly handed the file back to Matthew. *Seven days... seven sins. Time to break out the box again.*

"So what do you think? Do you choose to accept this mission?"

Silas winked before turning around and walking away. Matthew watched him disappear into the horizon before bowing his head. Silas was his last hope to redeem himself to Heaven. How could he re-claim his influential power, if he could sell free reign opportunity to Satan? He tucked the folder back into this jacket and stood up to walk away. With his pride hurt, he closed his eyes and prayed for a miracle. "Amen." He finally opened his eyes and smiled when he heard Silas' devilish voice echo the Mission Impossible Song throughout the heavenly sky.

"DOO DOO DOO-DOO DOO DOO DOO-DOO DOO DOO DOO-DOO DOO..."

9

DAY TWO
SO A MAN THINKETH

Mitchell stroked his neatly-groomed goatee as he stood in front of the still-misty bathroom mirror. A half-dressed woman lay across the bed in the luxurious penthouse suite.

"Leaving so soon?" she asked. "You really know how to hurt a woman's feelings."

"You know what this is. So don't try to make it anything else," Mitchell said. "You should be getting dressed too."

The woman rose from bed. "So, what are you going to do about the latest poll numbers?"

"I don't know. And with the election a week away, I really don't have a lot of time to figure it out." Mitchell said. "I've got to do something quick *and* decisive."

But nothing was going to get done as long as he lingered in that room. The office was where he needed to be.

"I've got to go," he said, adjusting his cufflinks. He kissed the woman and left to handle campaign business. "I'll send a car for you tonight when I'm ready to see you," he said in a tone that hinted the woman had no choice in the matter. "And speaking of cars, one's waiting for you downstairs. Make sure you get in it. I've left instructions with the driver as to what your responsibilities are for the day. No need to come into the office."

Several hours later, Mitchell was at his desk preparing to make the day's phone calls. A buzzer disturbed his work.

"I'm sorry to interrupt you, Mr. Rush," a woman's voice said. "There's a gentleman here who insists that he has an appointment with you. But he's not in your book OR on your calendar."

"It's okay, Serenity. I've been trying to reach him for weeks, and he finally had an opening for me today, so I set up a last-minute meeting with him."

"I understand, Sir," the woman said.

11

"I didn't have time to fill you in about it. I apologize. Please, kindly show the man in."

Before the woman could react, a burly man carrying a briefcase lumbered his way past her with a dismissive sweep of his hand. "Out of my way," he said, forcing the double doors open. He stepped in and then sat the briefcase down at his side.

The woman hurriedly followed, a pasted-on smile replacing her angered look.

Upon entering the office, they found themselves staring at Mitchell's back as he focused his attention to the bustling DC streets below the window of his huge corner office on Farragut Square. Behind him sat a massive cherry wood desk. He didn't bother to break his gaze, but simply motioned with his hand.

"Thank you, Serenity," he nodded, implying that he had nothing further for her. He slid away from the window.

The attentive assistant turned to leave, then she lingered an extra moment to address her boss. "Can I bring you anything,

Sir? Are there any files or documents I need to retrieve for your meeting?"

Mitchell finally turned around. "We're fine," he nodded.

"I'll leave you, then." Serenity headed towards the door, glancing behind her to get a good look at Mitchell's guest. She turned up her nose.

"And please close the doors behind you," Mitchell said. "We don't want to be interrupted." He stood up.

"In that case, Sir, may I take an early lunch? I'd like to run a few personal errands."

"That will be fine, Serenity. In fact, since this is my only meeting here in the office, take the rest of the day off."

"Thank you very much, Mr. Rush. I'll see you in the morning."

12   As the door slammed shut, Mitchell grabbed a bottle of his finest cognac from the stocked bar. He spoke.

"I told you never to come here, Silas," he chastised while pouring two glasses. He handed one to the burly man.

"Isn't it a bit early for libations?" Silas asked.

"Considering what I've been through the last six months, no it isn't."

"I'm just glad you finally called. I was beginning to wonder when you'd get serious about this presidential bid of yours," Silas Luxapher said with a smirk and a sip from his glass.

"I AM serious. I called you, didn't I?"

"And it's a good thing. Your poll numbers are down, the people don't trust you, and your own wife isn't even in your corner."

"*Must* you remind me of that?" Mitchell asked. He tossed the drink back in one gulp, and slammed the glass down on the desk.

"Someone has to," Silas snapped. "As you know, desperate situations call for desperate measures. And let's face it; with barely a week left until Election Day, I don't have to tell you that your situation is beyond desperate, Mitchell. It's dire."

Silas opened the briefcase to reveal its contents. He carefully picked the item up. "Take this," he said, handing it to Mitchell. "I have something you might be interested in. It could help with your current problem."

Mitchell stared at the exquisite antique box, its seven hinges rusted and creaking. He examined it in his hands, admiring the handiwork. It looked more like some ancient treasure from an Indiana Jones movie than something that would be useful in modern times.

"And exactly how is a *box* going to help me?" He asked as his face crooked with confusion.

Silas chuckled. "You know, everyone asks me that when I first offer the box to them. They wonder how such a small thing can help with their big problems. But when they realize what's inside and the power it holds, their skepticism quickly disappears. In fact, many are reluctant to relinquish the box once they've used it." Silas honed in on Mitchell's face. "Open it, Mitchell" he ordered. "We've got work to do."

The executive did as he was told. Mitchell peered into the box and was temporarily blinded by a flash of light. When his vision recovered, he counted the seven items inside, briefly handling each one, but not really understanding their relevance.

"How do I choose?" Mitchell asked.

"I don't know, but you must make a decision. And very soon. We have no time to waste-that's if you truly want to be elected President."

"What do you mean 'if'? My family, my reputation, my life's work so far, has all been tested during this campaign. I would not risk any of that on a whim! I want this more than anything!"

"Oh, I don't doubt that you want it, but what you're willing to do to get it? Now that's another matter altogether. And how

13

you handle your campaign from now until the election will give me that answer."

Mitchell perused the items in the box.

"Interesting," he said to the first one, shifting its position to get a good look at everything the box contained. "I've used this one many times," he laughed holding the second item. "Now this one...," he said, not finishing the sentence.

Mitchell held each of the seven deadly sins, wondering which would help him the most, and trying to envision how they would get him out of his current situation.

"Choose wisely," Silas, urged him. "There will be no time for second-guessing once the choice is made and the wheels are in motion."

"How many may I use?" he asked Silas.

14 "No more than two, but if you choose correctly, that's all you'll need. Be firm in your decision, and ready to follow through with your choice once you make it. You must commit to a course of action and stick with it once you've begun."

"Can I have a little time to think about this?"

"I'll stop back by around noon. And I'll need your decision then."

Mitchell showed Silas out and returned to his desk to ponder how he would make his decision. He began doing paperwork, but eventually he dozed off and slipped into a dream.

As he reached REM sleep, his mind wandered back to a few years ago when he first discussed running for President of the United States with his wife. She was totally in his corner back then.

"I think you'd do a lot of great things for the country," he remembered her saying. "You're a good man. I'd vote for you," she winked.

Mitchell smiled. *That woman's always been in my corner*, he concluded. Even his subconscious knew that.

But that seemed like a million years ago. There was so much distance between him and his wife now.

Mitchell chalked it up to how busy he was with the campaign, but deep down, he knew it was totally his fault. He'd done this, and as much as he wished he could go back, he realized being elected president would only make matters worse. They'd spend even less time together, and the demands placed upon him by the new job would pull apart the already-weakened fibers of his marriage.

Still, he *had* to be president, even if his wife turned out to be the first casualty of his victory.

To the victor goes the spoils, he thought as memories of happier days made him smile in his sleep.

He remembered how they met...

She was working at an on-campus voter registration drive at Bowie State. Dressed in jeans, a white t-shirt, and sandals, she approached Mitchell, who was in his last year of law school at Georgetown.

"DC, huh? I know *you're* registered to vote, right?"

"And if I'm not?"

"Then you'll need one of these," she said, handing him a card. "Fill it out and give it back to me. We'll make sure you're all set for this upcoming election. Here's a pen."

Mitchell took the card, completed it, and handed it back to her. He had circled his phone number.

"I'm sorry, Sir," she replied. "Some of your information is hard to read. Can you fill out another card? Legibly this time, please?"

Before handing him the card, she put her number on it with a note. *You call me*, the note read.

Mitchell accepted the card, read the note, and smiled. "Can I complete this and bring it back? I'm running late for an important meeting."

15

"I'll bet. Well, we'll be here all week," the young woman said. She winked.

He knew then that she was the type of woman he wanted in his life. She was feisty, but Mitchell could tell that if he somehow managed to break through her tough exterior, she would be all in. And without question, he needed a woman like her to achieve the goals he'd set for himself.

Mitchell remembered how they dated for a year, and then married a few weeks after he passed the bar exams in both Maryland and DC.

Still lost in his power nap at the office, he smiled again as flashes from their wedding played in his dreams like a video in HD.

They settled into a modest starter home, and Mitchell went into private practice for a few years, making a name for himself in their local community of Baltimore. He put his support behind a few pieces of important legislation, organized a group of Habitat for Humanity volunteers, and his office sponsored an after school learning center near where he grew up. Remarkably, Mitchell did all this while still running the law firm.

That was just the beginning.

After serving on several community boards and making a few local contacts with far-reaching influence, Mitchell was on the fast track to politics at the national level. He and his wife moved from Baltimore to Washington DC. That year, they were invited to all the events necessary to get a man noticed, and before long, Mitchell Rush found himself deeply entrenched in the powerful machine that was DC politics. The environment was ripe with the potential of connections that would definitely put a man in all the right circles. A little elbow-rubbing with the elite and he'd be on his way. Mitchell decided to take advantage of the opportunity that he felt he'd earned. He rolled up his sleeves, stayed active and visible, and in just a few months, he knew all the important movers and shakers in both the political and legal arenas by their first names. He received national attention when he was recognized for his work on a class action suit against builders who used substandard materials in low-income housing near his old neighborhood.

"Not bad for a kid from the wrong side of the tracks in B'more, huh?" his wife had whispered while standing next to him on the stage waiting to receive the prestigious award.

"You've always supported me," he whispered to her as the crowd looked on.

Mitchell was no fool. While he knew he had earned that award with his hard work, he also knew that his wife played an enormous role in his winning it. Having that smart, beautiful, and confident woman by his side was turning out to be the best move he'd made. It was what had propelled him to the next level. If Mitchell was the total package, his wife was definitely the wrapping and the bow that made the whole package more attractive. Together, they would be unstoppable.

But his world came crashing down when after a one-night office fling, Mitchell came home and confessed.

17

"She means nothing to me, baby," he said, trying to explain his foolish actions to his wife.

He thought she bought into it initially, but things were never the same between them after that.

Mitchell felt horrible about the bind he had put his wife in and how he risked his marriage. He couldn't believe that he'd shattered his wife's trust for a damn stranger. For him, it was such an unfair trade. His wife was devastated.

Mitchell vowed never to stray again and, after counseling and a few concessions, his wife took him back.

He was grateful for that.

"I thank God every day that you stayed with me," Mitchell said a few weeks after the incident. He tenderly kissed the woman who'd been by his side since law school.

"And you're damned lucky I did," she said. "Don't you forget that." She smiled at him. "You know I love you, right?"

No response was needed. Mitchell knew that her love showed in all she did, everything she put up with. And he was the one who had taken that for granted to be with a woman he'd just met.

Not long after that, he declared his intent to run for POTUS and quickly earned his party's nomination. They left his fling in the past, and the two of them worked side-by-side to give Mitchell the best chance of winning.

But it's a long way from public housing in Cherry Hill to a corner office on Farragut Square just blocks from the White House, and an even longer one to the highest elected position in the land. And while Mitchell understood there would be *some* give and take, he found himself doing a little too much of both: *giving in* on issues that were important to him, and *taking* a lot of crap from people who weren't nearly as smart or as connected as he was.

18 The hammer fell again when Mitchell engaged in an affair.

Unlike that tawdry hook-up with the office tramp, from the very beginning, this woman wanted more than Mitchell could give. He was flattered that she was willing to leave her husband to be with him. His ego loved that, but he had no plans to leave his wife. He thought the woman was clear on that from the first night.

It lasted for almost a year. Mitchell never thought his wife would find out.

"And even if she does," he boasted to Sonny. "I can handle her."

But when his wife received a series of photos via text and videos in e-mail, instead of confronting Mitchell and handling things behind closed doors, she went straight to the media.

"I can't believe he's done this to me again! We've been together since college!" she bellowed into the camera. "I've had enough of his womanizing!"

Mitchell was caught off guard later that day during a press conference.

"Have you spoken with your wife today, Mr. Rush?" one reporter asked. "Have you seen the news?"

"Is it true that you've been having an affair?" another reporter asked. "And it isn't your first one, is it, Mr. Rush?"

The public unveiling of such a private issue angered Mitchell. He decided then and there that he would get revenge on the person he believed was responsible.

It never occurred to him to look in the mirror.

Instead, he wallowed in the humiliation of having the affair exposed publicly by his own wife. Oblivious to the real issue, Mitchell was more concerned with how things went public than the fact that he'd cheated in the first place.

Realizing his wife might need some space, Mitchell moved out of the 10-room Tudor home and into the penthouse.

"And don't tell people that I threw you out, Mitchell," she said as he packed. "Because that's not true. Your selfishness is why we need to live apart for a while."

She promised to discuss staying in the marriage past the election, but only after a visit to her attorneys, a visit that included making some sizeable "adjustments" to the payoff agreement she had drafted after Mitchell's first indiscretion.

Mitchell gave her what she wanted because he didn't have time to argue in the middle of his campaign and he didn't need the extra press. Plus, he felt he owed it to her to try and make things right.

Besides, he knew he would never be elected without her. They *had* to present a united front, even if only in public. Mitchell decided that since he'd be spending so much time working anyway, getting a penthouse in the city would be the perfect solution. And it gave him a way to explain why he and his wife were living at separate addresses. He would blame it all on the campaign.

"I'll support your run for the White House because you've worked so hard for it," she said. "But it's going to cost you much more than money to convince me to share that presidential bedroom with you in Washington. You've had your last freebie."

Mitchell awoke with tears in his eyes.

How could I have been so stupid?

He checked his watch and noticed that more than an hour had passed.

Silas will be back for his answer soon, he thought.

He glanced down at his shoes.

I really need to shine these, he thought just as the phone rang.

"Hey, man," Sonny said. What you doin'?"

"I'm about to shine my shoes," Mitchell said.

"Seriously, Mitch? You're in line for the presidency of the United States and you can't find nobody to polish your shoes? You want me to come pick them up? They have concierge services in the lobby. Why don't you just take them down there?"

"You know what? This is one of the things that I still enjoy doing myself. I've always taken pride in polishing my own shoes and that won't change. Not even when I'm in the White House."

"You say that *now*," Sonny replied.

Jackson "Sonny" Styles was Mitch's oldest and most trusted friend. The two men had known each other since they were boys playing in the Pop Warner football league back in Baltimore. Thick as thieves all through high school, they separated briefly, when Sonny joined the military. After two enlistments, Sonny came home, and Mitchell convinced him to be a part of his rise to the White House. He told Sonny it wouldn't be the same without his lead blocker out in front clearing the way. His duties would include Mitchell's scheduling, getting him where he needed to be, and taking care of all the loose ends that came up. Sonny eagerly signed on and he had worked for Mitchell ever since.

"I know I have expensive cars, designer shoes, a beautiful woman, and all the trappings of the good life," Mitchell said. "But I'm still that same guy from back in the day, man. Nothing's changed. And it won't."

"So you're really going to shine your own shoes, huh?"

Once his punishment as a child, Mitchell had come to appreciate the focus and humility involved with the seemingly menial task of polishing shoes. In his teens, he loved having people comment on how shiny his shoes were and he carried that into adulthood. It made him stand out at an early age, and even now, it was the one thing he did when he needed to clear his mind while making a major decision.

And the decision before him definitely fit *that* bill.

As Mitchell prepared to buff the five hundred dollar oxfords to polished perfection, his mind flashed back to a conversation he'd had with his grandfather many years ago.

21

"You can tell a lot about a man by his shoes, and how he takes care of them," the preacher used to say when Mitchell's shoes weren't exactly up to par.

I really miss you, Old Man, Mitchell mumbled. I sure could use your wisdom right now.

He bowed his head.

There was a knock on the door.

"Hey, Sonny," he said. "Let me get back to you, man. I gotta' wrap up this important meeting. Then I'm done here for the day."

"Cool, but don't forget I'll be picking you up this afternoon for your ride through downtown as the presidential candidate. The local supporters can get their last up-close glimpse of Mitchell Rush before he takes his place on the national stage. We can shake some hands, take some photos, you know, rally the voters for the homestretch."

"I won't forget. Call me later with all the details," Mitchell said.

"I will," Sonny said.

Mitchell hung up the phone and addressed the visitor outside his office door.

"Come in," Mitchell said.

Silas entered. "So have you made your decision, Mitchell? Am I looking at the next President of the United States or what?" he asked. "Are you ready to play dirty?"

At that very moment, Mitchell's conscience gave in. He had finally realized that it would take much more than just his squeaky-clean image and his past good deeds to propel him to the job he would kill to have. The way he looked at it, poor decision-making had put him here, and he would not miss out on a golden opportunity to counter those missteps with what Silas offered.

"Give me the damn box," Mitchell snapped. He opened it. Nestled between Greed and Lust, his eyes were immediately drawn to Pride. "I'll take this one, he said. "And Envy will be the perfect backup."

"Decisive and enthusiastic. I'm impressed. Those are definitely qualities that a president needs. Congratulations on taking your destiny into your own hands. You may use the items as you wish to achieve your goal," Silas informed him. "No boundaries, no rules."

"NO rules?"

"That's right. Just remember, you choose the sin, you deal with the consequences. *Whatever* they are. But I guarantee that whatever you choose, it will bring you your heart's desire. You *will* become President of the United States. And everything that comes with it will be yours."

That was exactly what Mitchell wanted to hear, what he *needed* to hear. It had been such a long road and Mitchell could see the finish line, although recent stumbles on his part made it seem like the closer he got to his dream, the further away it became.

22

But now that he had Silas' secret weapons, all of that was about to change.

Mitchell couldn't believe his fortune. It seemed too good to be true.

"So what's in it for you?" Mitchell asked Silas.

"Absolutely nothing. For now. You're a politician, so you understand that having a man in high places who owes you favors isn't exactly a bad thing. In fact, it can actually come in handy from time to time. And before you ask, I'm no different from any other supporter in that I'll just be one of the many who helped you ascend to the Oval Office. And when I call in my chips, I'm sure I can count on you to deliver just as you will with the others who helped you get there."

In Mitchell's mind, he'd already promised more to people who, in the end, did nothing for him at all. To him, just the guarantee that he would be president was more than worth it- no matter what "it" turned out to be.

23

Sounds fair, Mitchell thought. He extended his hand to Silas.

Silas responded with his own firm handshake and a pat on Mitchell's shoulder.

"I'll take my leave, then," Silas said. He picked up the box, counted the remaining sins, and gently closed the box. He tapped Mitchell's back on the way out of the office. "Good luck," he said.

"Thanks," Mitchell said. "But if what you say is true, I won't need luck. I've got everything I need right here." He picked up the items and held them. "It's going to be great working with you as a partner, Silas."

Unfortunately for him, Mitchell had no idea what he had gotten himself into by accepting Silas' help. As for being 'partners,' Mitchell had it all twisted; to Silas, they would never be partners because they weren't equals since Mitchell didn't know the truth about who he was really dealing with.

Silas Luxapher wasn't like the other people to whom Mitchell would owe favors: ordinary folks who would settle for a nod on legislation or for his support of some cause. He was a man with sinister intentions and ulterior motives who never did anything for anyone without expecting something in return.

And for many, the price proved to be too high.

But Silas didn't consider that *his* problem. The way he looked at it, he was a savvy negotiator who provided a service; opportunities and options when there seemed to be none. In return, he simply charged a price comparable to the value of what he was able to deliver. "Big dreams have big price tags," he always said. "I'm just a businessman," he would delude himself.

But in actuality, Silas was nothing more than a master manipulator whose specialty was dealing in half-truths and preying on the weak. Those with ambition and a lack of conscience were ideal customers for him because the less of a conscience a person had, the more susceptible they were to his schemes. And the really driven ones were so focused on getting what they wanted that they never asked any questions upfront.

24

It was perfect arrangement.

Silas would offer to help with whatever problem the person was facing, but he never divulged what it would actually cost them until after the problem was resolved. That's when he would go in for the kill. This way, he always made sure the poor unsuspecting soul was so caught up in getting what they wanted that the price didn't matter. They'd pay anything. And even if they wanted to balk, by then, it was too late to renege on the deal they had struck with him.

The unfortunate sap was indebted to him for life.

And everyone paid Silas what they owed him...or else.

Shortly after Silas left, Mitchell packed his briefcase.

"Can't forget these," he said, grabbing the items he just received from his new ally.

Mitchell locked the office and headed home ready to handle whatever the next week had in store for him. Silas' gifts gave him confidence that he could get away with anything. Mitchell strutted all the way to the parking garage, excited that his dream was within his grasp, and that in less than seven days, he would be President of the United States.

As he drove, Mitchell remembered that it was the affair that really threw things off course in his marriage. For some reason, lately, it seemed that he couldn't please his wife. She was able to see right through him.

"You've changed so much from that man I knew before this campaign," she'd say. "You're different. And I'm not sure I like the man you're becoming."

"What do you mean, I'm *different?*"

"For one, it seems like you've begun to believe your own press. I often wonder what happened to that humble man I married. The man who spoke from the heart," she said. These days, your conversation is more like a series of snappy made-for-CNN sound bites crafted by your PR person, even when you talk to me. I'm not a constituent, Mitchell. I'm your wife, the woman who was with you before all this."

"Honey," Mitchell said." You know the press is everywhere. And with everyone trying to trip me up, I have to be ready for anything. They're always shoving microphones in my face; I'm being watched night and day. Hell, the only peace and quiet I get is when I'm at the office."

"And at the penthouse, apparently," his wife interjected, her voice dripping with venom and cynicism.

"If I could move back home, I wouldn't have to spend so much time there."

"Oh, so it's my fault that you're living there?"

"You know that's not what I'm saying, baby."

"Well, that's what it sounds like."

"Can we not talk about this now, please?" Mitchell asked. Clenching his teeth, he realized he would not win this argument if it continued the way it was currently going. "I promise you, when the election is over, things will be different." He leaned in to kiss his wife. She pulled away.

He hoped the promise would pacify her for the moment, but he knew full well what the *real* issue was: those damn pictures and that video! Without those, his marriage would not be on the rocks right now.

Mitchell always planned to destroy Franklin Tolliver, the man who sent them, but until now, he had no idea how he'd make that happen. With all of his talents and abilities, he was ill-equipped to fight this battle alone. He knew that.

But he *had* to do something because as far as he was concerned, revenge was critical to setting the tone for his impending presidency. And if Silas was able to provide a means to *that* end, Mitchell wasn't going to refuse the help. That box and Silas were what he'd prayed for the last few months.

26

When Mitchell left that second meeting with Silas, he was encouraged and sure of two things: that *he* would be president, and that vengeance would be dealt.

But he wasn't the only one plotting revenge.

A man he'd never met knew about the suite that the campaign had leased for "meetings." He also knew it was the one time that Mitchell's security team would be lax, as only Sonny was on duty those evenings when post-dinner "discussions" were needed.

The man would wait for Mitchell to come to the spot with what he assumed would be another conquest and he would do the job he was being paid very well to do.

"We need Mitchell Rush eliminated," he was told. "His vision for the country doesn't fall in line with our goals."

Then a large briefcase of cash was presented. "Half now and half when our candidate is sworn into office," they said.

The man didn't ask for details because he didn't need to know them. Nor did he want to have that kind of information, since it would only get him killed. The less he knew, the better it was for him. He agreed to take the job with all its risks.

Mitchell Rush would be handled.

And there was *at least* one woman who had her own plans for the philandering would-be President of the United States.

"Frankly, I'm glad it's out," she said when news of their affair broke. "Now we can be together."

"Together?" Mitchell asked with a puzzled look. "I'm not leaving my wife! I love her!"

"Oh, like you've been *loving* ME the last couple of months? Mitchell, she's made it crystal clear that she doesn't want to be with you. Why would you hold on to her when you have me? We could move into the White House together once your divorce is final. Maybe even have the wedding in the presidential garden."

This chick must be crazy, Mitchell thought to himself at the time and he didn't even bother to respond to her ridiculous ramblings about marriage. Instead, he cut off all ties with the woman, banned her from campaign headquarters, and reluctantly looked into getting a restraining order against her.

"I don't need the press, Sonny."

"I know you don't, but what if she tries to hurt your wife, Mitch? She could come after her. This is the quickest way to get 'psycho-chick' in check."

But it was also the quickest to make her angry, a fact that Mitchell never considered. So at Sonny's urging, he went ahead and filed the necessary papers, claiming the woman was some psycho who latched on to him for no reason at all. It worked and Mitchell felt safer after he'd done it.

"You're going to be sorry you ever chose her over me," the woman screamed when the order was served to her at home.

27

She picked up her phone. "The bastard has the nerve to break up with *me?*"

"Hey, let's not get distracted," a strong voice said on the other end. "Mitchell Rush will get what's coming to him. But we *must* stay focused on the big picture, and remember why we're doing this."

"You have your reasons and I have mine," the scorned woman said.

Somewhere in an abandoned building across town, a cell phone rang. A man answered.

"So are you ready to put in some work?"

"Absolutely, but I'll need a few things," the man said.

"We'll get you everything you need. You just handle Rush, and we'll take care of the rest," a voice said.

"Consider it done," the man replied.

"We really appreciate your help in this. Your devotion will be handsomely rewarded once our guy is sworn in. Get in a cab. I'll call you with additional instructions. Just remember the cause in all this."

Truth is, the man didn't really give a damn about any 'cause'; he was only interested in a payday that would set him up for life. To him, a job was a job. And, considering the magnitude of his latest assignment, he was going to make sure he was paid well enough to retire after it was done. If all went well, Mitchell Rush would be dead by the end of the week and the hit man would be somewhere soaking up the sun surrounded by beautiful women and endless rounds of bottomless drinks.

Nothing personal, Mr. Rush. This is strictly business, the hired hand said to himself. *It seems the wrong people feel you're not the best man for the job.*

Now on his way with Silas' tools at his disposal, Mitchell made a few stops and then went back to the penthouse to rest for the evening's events. He was about to doze off when Sonny called.

"Hey, man," Mitchell said. "Have you thought anymore about what we discussed earlier? You got any details for handling Tolliver tonight?"

"So you're really going through with this?" Sonny asked his friend.

"I have to. I guess deep down, I'm still that kid from the neighborhood with something to prove," Mitchell said. "And that kid would never put up with being disrespected."

"But you're *not* that kid, man! You're running for President of the United States. So you can't go around acting like we're still running up and down those streets in Cherry Hill! Let some of that shit go, Mitchell! Get your head focused on the *end game!*"

"I can't, Sonny."

"You know," Sonny said. "We have people in place to handle these types of things for you, man. Hell, I'll take care of it myself if you need me to."

"I hear you," Mitchell said. "And I appreciate your loyalty. But I want to see the look on that bastard's face when I call him on what he did. I want him to *know* that no one humiliates Mitchell Rush! No one! I'm about to be President of the United States, damn it!"

"Not if you get caught," Sonny warned.

"You know what? I need you to do what I pay you to do. You should just have my back, man and help me get this done. No more talking about it, Sonny. Either you're in with me on this, or you're out of a job, and I'll find someone who I can trust to do what needs to be done! I thought that person was you, but maybe I was wrong about that. Was I wrong, Sonny?"

Sonny couldn't believe that Mitchell went there with him after all the years they had known each other, but Mitchell was right, he had to help his friend who was more like a brother to him.

"No, you weren't wrong, man. I got you like always."

29

"Well then, we've got to figure out a way to have me in two places at one time," Mitchell said.

"Or at least make it *look* like you are," Sonny replied.

"Now you're talking, man," Mitchell said. He fist-bumped his friend. "So what car am I riding in this afternoon?"

"The Hummer limo."

"It has really dark tint right?"

"Yep."

"Okay. That might work," Mitchell said.

"Let me see what I can come up with. I'll get back to you," Sonny said.

"I've got a few loose ends to tie up anyway," Mitchell said.

It wasn't long before Sonny called Mitchell. "I think I've got an idea," he said. "Meet me at the penthouse in one hour."

Sonny arrived at the suite with another man.

"What do you think?" Sonny asked.

"Hmmm, it could work," Mitchell replied, giving his stamp of approval to the last phase of his plan for revenge.

"I need one of your shirts, Mitch. One of those expensive business shirts."

"In the closet," Mitch said. "On the right."

"Come with me," Sonny told the other man who could have easily passed for Mitchell's brother, if he'd had one. They walked into the immense wardrobe closet. *Some folks have bedrooms smaller than this*, Sonny thought as he picked out a shirt.

"Take whatever you need. I'm sure there's something here that'll fit him."

"You go ahead and get ready for what you gotta' do, Mitch," Sonny instructed. "We'll be headed out of here in a few. Remember to time your thing to coincide with our appearance. You'll have about an hour and a half from the time we start rolling. Handle that business, then you need to go somewhere and be seen. The more public, the better."

"Got it."

Thirty minutes later, Mitchell's limo cruised down the middle of K Street. Between 15th and 20th Streets, people lined up on both sides hoping to see Mitchell Rush, maybe even shake his hand before they cast their votes for him.

"Mr. Rush, Mr. Rush," they yelled from behind the barriers set up by police.

The limo stopped at 17th Street and the rear passenger window of the Hummer rolled down slightly. It was just enough for a right hand and arm to be revealed. A monogrammed sleeve with the letters "M.R." was seen, and Mitchell's signature platinum cufflinks gleamed as the hand waved. The window rolled back up.

Sonny got out of the limo to address the small crowd that had gathered. Not much could be seen through the tinted windows of the vehicle.

31

"Back it up, people! Behind the barriers, please."

The crowd complied. Sonny spoke.

"Thank you all for your support. We'll celebrate together later this week when it's official. This isn't over yet. There's still work to do until we cross the finish line. Thank you so much."

"Can we have a few words from Mr. Rush?"

"Unfortunately, not right now. He has to go."

The window rolled down briefly and there was another wave from the limo before it pulled off to continue the drive through downtown.

Meanwhile, on the other side of town, the *real* Mitchell was putting his plan for revenge in motion.

Mitch had sent someone to pick Tolliver up for the meeting, a meeting Tolliver believed would get him paid for the photos and video he was threatening to release.

"Get in," the driver said when Frank showed up at the appointed place.

The blackmailer climbed in. Mitchell was already inside. They spoke briefly as the car took off.

"I'm glad you finally realize what a tenuous situation you're in, Mitchell," Frank said, settling into the back seat.

"*Tenuous*, huh? That's a big word for you, isn't it?" Mitchell asked. "Do you *really* think I'm going to sit here and be blackmailed by some thug with a high school diploma?"

"I don't see that you have a choice," Tolliver said. "Pay the money or suffer the consequences."

"You see, that's where you're wrong. I have a few other options. Besides, if I pay you, my reputation and everything I've worked for will be shot to hell. And you'll never stop hitting me up for money. I would never be free."

32

"But at least you'd be president. Isn't that what you want more than anything? Even at the expense of your marriage?"

"You know what, Frank? When this is all over, I'm going to have my wife *and* the presidency! Once I'm elected, the smoke will clear from these alleged 'new photos' you have that no one will ever see and I'll be able to deal with my wife. But it all begins with getting rid of you!"

Mitchell pulled out a vial and syringe. He drew a small amount of a clear liquid into the syringe, and plunged the needle into Tolliver's arm. Mitchell thought his victim would pass out, but Tolliver remained conscious. He was babbling.

"You won't get away with this, Mitchell!" Tolliver said. Fear showed in his eyes as he began to sense the end.

The car stopped in an alley.

"Get out, Frank," Mitchell said. He pushed him. "Keep the car running and wait here," he told the driver.

With Mitchell supporting the bulk of Tolliver's weight, the two men walked towards an old warehouse. Mitchell pulled out a gun.

"Where are the pictures?" Mitchell asked as he shoved the gun in Frank's back.

"You'll never find them especially if you kill me."

"No ifs about it. You're going to die," Mitchell said. "Turn around, I wanna' look you in the eye when I kill you."

"The voters have no idea the man they're getting as president," Tolliver barked.

"And you'll never live long enough to tell them. Now, about those pictures...are you going to tell me where they are?" Mitchell asked. He paused before continuing. "Last chance to save your life."

Frank didn't respond.

"Give me your phone," Mitchell said as he reached into one of Frank's pockets with his left hand while holding the gun in his right. "What's this?" he asked, feeling what turned out to be a loose SD card.

33

With both of Mitchell's hands now occupied, Tolliver saw this as his chance to resist. He grabbed the barrel of the gun, and the two men struggled to gain control of it. A shot went off, hitting Tolliver in the stomach. He bent over at the waist and coughed. Blood spewed out.

Mitchell jumped back, causing Frank to fall to the ground. A few droplets of blood hit the top of Mitchell's shoes.

"Damn it!" he said. "You ruined my shoes, you bastard!" He fired again, this time into Tolliver's head.

Hearing the second gunshot, Mitchell's driver came running.

"Is everything okay, Mr. Rush?" The gun was still in Mitchell's hand.

"I'm fine," Mitchell answered, although he was shaking.

"Give me the gun," the driver said. "What should we do with the body, Sir?"

"I'd rather keep the gun myself," Mitchell said. "I don't want it to end up in the wrong hands. As for the body, leave it here. I want him to be found tonight."

When he thought about what just happened, Mitchell's shoulders lifted. His revenge was complete.

"Let's get back to the car," the driver said.

As they walked away from Frank's body, Mitchell looked down at his feet, reminded that the shoes had been stained.

"Maybe you should get rid of those, Sir," the driver said.

"Good idea."

They stopped by the shoe store to purchase a new pair of shoes.

"I'd like to wear these out if I could," he told the saleswoman while paying for them. "Can I have an extra bag for the ones I wore into the store?"

"Certainly, Sir. May I put them in the bag for you?" she said, reaching out her hands.

"That's alright," Mitchell said. "I'll just take the bag." He put the bloody shoes inside.

"Would you like me to stop by a dumpster so we can toss those, Sir?"

"On second thought, I think I'll keep them. They're my favorite pair of Moreschi calfskins and cost over nine hundred dollars. Just take me home. I'll figure out what to do with them later."

"Yes, Sir."

Back at the penthouse, Mitchell made a beeline to the large custom shoe closet of the master suite. Organized boxes of expensive shoes lined one entire wall, each pair shelved in its own nook. Many of the shoes had been made especially for Mitchell. Along another wall, boxes were stacked sideways end-to-end. There had to be close to one hundred pairs of shoes in the closet.

He removed the stained shoes from the bag and attempted to wipe them down. He examined them closely.

Looks like I got most of it. I'll hit them again later. Right now, I have other pressing issues.

Mitchell found an empty box and put the bloody shoes inside. He tucked the syringe and vial in one shoe and the gun in another before closing the box. Then he slid the box to the back of the closet, stacking a row of boxes in front of it. He grabbed two brand new boxes from the shelves and put them into bags. He headed to the hall to wait for the elevator.

Seven days and counting, he told himself as the doors opened. He disappeared behind them.

When the elevator stopped, Mitchell stepped out, whistling as he strutted through the lobby. He was in a great mood.

Frank was dead. It seemed like things were going to be alright after all.

35

Mitchell picked up speed until he reached the concierge desk.

"Is there someone here to shine these shoes?" He asked the concierge.

The man at the desk pointed him in the direction of a massive door with a window at waist height. The door swung inward. Mitchell entered and tossed two boxes of shoes at the old man behind the counter. The lids fell off the boxes.

A teenager looked on.

"Shine these, Old Timer," he said.

"You got it. You gonna' wait for them?"

"I have things to do. I'll be back later tonight to pick them up."

"They'll be ready." He paused to get a good look at Mitchell. "Hey, I know you. Aren't you that fella' whose wife was crying on TV awhile back?" he asked. "Pretty lady. Too pretty to be crying."

"Listen old man, I'm not here for conversation, just to drop off the shoes. I used to shine them myself, but I'm too busy these days - don't have time for such trivial things anymore. So get to work, and do a good job. Those are the shoes of the next President of the United States."

"I take pride in my work and always do a good job, but I'll put an extra-special shine on these, so you'll look real spiffy on election night," the old man said as he opened one of the boxes. He removed the shoes.

The old man took out his rag and laid out the other tools of his trade. He began his work.

"Grab that other pair," he told the young apprentice, sliding the second box to him.

36   "Dang! These shoes cost a fortune!" the teen exclaimed, holding the box. "The price tag's still on them. I can't believe somebody can afford to spend *that* much on one pair of shoes! You're a baller, huh?" he asked, turning toward Mitchell.

"Young man, you're wasting time talking when you should be shining those shoes," Mitchell said in a condescending tone. "And be careful. You've seen how much they cost, so you know you can't afford to replace them."

Mitchell left the lobby and hit the streets for a little impromptu mingling with the voters.

"What an asshole," the teenage boy mumbled as Mitchell walked off.

Mitchell headed down 17th Street and turned onto H Street. At the corner of 16th and H, he stopped at a diner to grab a bite to eat. It didn't take long for word to circulate that Mitchell Rush was in the area. A crowd from Lafayette Park came over to the diner to meet him.

"Wow, I can't believe the future president buys his own sandwich. It's like he's a regular guy," someone said.

In the middle of the crowd, a beautiful, curvaceous woman caught Mitchell's eye. He winked at her. She spoke.

"So *you're* Mitchell Rush, huh? The news stories about you don't do you justice. You're very handsome."

Mitchell was flattered.

"Mr. Rush, here among the common people. Imagine that," the woman said.

"Are you a supporter, Ma'am?" Mitchell asked. "Will you be voting for Team Rush?"

"I'm among the undecided voters who could swing the election one way or the other. It all depends on what I hear this week."

"Really? *Still* undecided this late in the game? Clearly, you haven't been paying attention to what I plan to do once I'm in the White House."

37

Mitchell left the woman to converse and mingle for about an hour. In that time, the media had gathered. A small crew came inside the diner to capture the event for the evening news. The diner owner appreciated the traffic, which translated into dollars and cents in sales.

"Well, I'd better go everybody. Big week ahead," Mitchell said after a few questions from the crowd. "See you all at the victory party exactly seven days from now."

Before he left, Mitchell went over to the woman and whispered. "Perhaps I can explain my plan for the country to you in private," Mitchell said. "What are you doing after this?"

"I doubt you can swing my vote your way in one evening."

"I'm very convincing. Just ask everybody at my campaign headquarters and all the folks who have already committed to voting for me."

"Well, I'm a bit harder to convince than most. I follow my own mind."

"I drove my car here. What about you? Did you come here alone?"

"I took a cab," the woman said. "And yes, I'm alone tonight."

"Well, one call and a car will pick you up."

"Guess you better make that call then." The chemistry between them was apparent.

Mitchell stepped out of the room to dial his cell phone.

"It's on the way," he told the woman a few minutes later. "I'll meet you at my penthouse. And bring a change of clothes. You're staying the night."

"Okay, then it's a date. I need to make a call and cancel some plans I made earlier."

"Just jump in the limo when it gets here. That's *if* you don't change your mind."

38

"I'm a woman of my word. I'll be there. Just make sure you haven't changed *your* mind."

An hour later, Mitchell buzzed the woman into his suite. All he wore was satin sleeping pants.

"Well, come in," he said. "Guess you really are a woman of your word."

The woman entered the suite and sat down her bag.

"Make yourself comfortable. Would you like something to drink?" Mitchell asked her.

"The way you're dressed, it looks like drinking is the last thing on your mind," the seductress replied. "Where's your bathroom?" she asked. "I'd like to freshen up."

"Through the living room and to your right. It's the second door."

"I won't be long." She grabbed her bag.

"I'll make you that drink while I wait. You strike me as an Apple Martini kind of woman."

"Very perceptive," the woman said. She headed towards the bathroom.

Mitchell mixed the perfect Appletini and poured himself a glass of cognac. He sat patiently on the sofa.

The woman returned from the bathroom wearing an amazingly sexy black teddy with matching robe. Thigh-high sheer black stockings and black stilettos complemented all she had to offer a man. Mitchell was stunned.

"What do you think?" she asked. She spun around so Mitchell could give her the 360 degree once-over.

"Wow," he said, his mouth hanging wide open. "You've definitely got *my* vote."

"You're the one who's running for office," she said. "So now that we're in private, convince me that you're the man for the job."

"Let's take this to the bedroom," Mitchell said.

39

He took the woman by the hand and led her to the wing of the penthouse reserved for the master suite. Along the main wall, a round California King bed with its custom leather headboard served as the centerpiece of the room. An imported Italian nightstand framed the bed on each side. Trey ceilings gave the room a Sistine Chapel feel.

Mitchell picked the woman up and laid her in the middle of the bed. He crawled up next to her.

"No more talk about voting or anything related to work," he said, taking a few moments to admire the woman. He gently touched the straps of her teddy to kiss each shoulder.

"Your lips feel amazing," the woman said with her eyes closed. "Who knew such a powerful man could be so sensual?"

"So you find power sexy, huh?"

"Doesn't every woman?"

"I think some are intimidated by it," Mitchell answered, working his way down her body.

"But I'm not one of those women. Power turns me on."

Before they could get into anything more intense, Mitchell's phone rang.

"Is that one of your many women calling?"

Mitchell picked up the phone. Sonny was on the line.

"Turn on the news, Mitch," Sonny said. "You've got to see this!"

Mitchell grabbed the remote and turned the channel to the 11:00 p.m. news.

"Rebounding from a lull in recent weeks, it seems that Mitchell Rush's poll numbers may be on the upswing," the news anchor said.

Footage from the diner played on the screen. The crowd cheered as Mitchell addressed them.

40 Mitchell stepped away to talk to Sonny. He tossed the remote on the bed. "I told you things would turn around!"

While Mitchell's attention was focused on Sonny's call, a breaking story flashed across the screen.

The body of Franklin Tolliver has just been found.

"Oh my God!" the woman said.

"What's wrong?"

"Something about a Frank Tolliver just crawled across the screen!"

"Sonny, I gotta' go!"

Mitchell ran back to the bed to see what the woman was talking about. A reporter was standing near Mitchell's office.

"Turn that up," he told her. He didn't want to miss a word.

"We're here outside Rush headquarters with a breaking story. It seems that earlier today, while the rest of the city was celebrating the rise of Presidential Candidate and native son Mitchell Rush, Frank Tolliver was being murdered by an unknown assailant. If you remember, he's the man who recently came forward as the one who obtained the infamous video footage of Rush with his mistress, the same video that Rush's wife turned over to the media. That was six months ago and while no one knows how he got the video, it's caused quite a firestorm since it was released. Frank Tolliver recently threatened to release even more damning pictures if Rush didn't pay him. And now he's dead."

Mitchell stared at the television screen.

"At least they didn't imply that I had something to do with that man's death," Mitchell said.

"Did he *really* try to hit you up for money?" the woman asked.

"Only via the media, but I didn't have time to respond to his ridiculous attempts to get attention for himself. I'm busy with my campaign and gearing up to run this country."

"Well, I'm just glad you were someplace else."

"So am I."

Mitchell was on such a high, but he couldn't exactly celebrate Frank's death without raising public eyebrows, and he didn't want to speak ill of the dead, even if the man had been blackmailing him. So he decided to release a statement through his PR team in the morning and just leave it at that.

Still, political correctness aside, Mitchell was absolutely beaming with joy because, thanks to Silas and the antique box, his pride had been restored. In his mind, the foundation for his presidency had been set. It had turned out to be a great day. His numbers were surging at the right time, and as a bonus, he had taught his enemies that he was not to be crossed.

But Mitchell hadn't learned any lessons of his own because here he was, spending time with yet another woman when his wife had already given him more chances than he deserved. On the heels of that last affair, Mitchell had promised to do his part to fix his marriage, but those words were forgotten the moment that the next short skirt caught his eye. He just couldn't help

41

himself; when it came to women, Mitchell got what he wanted with little work on his part. And he made a point of going after the married ones just to prove he could have what belonged to another man. For him, it was more about boosting his ego than anything else.

"Hey, I'm sorry, but you've got to get out of here," he told the woman whose name he didn't care to remember. He handed her two one-hundred dollar bills. "That's for your time. There's a car waiting for you downstairs. And make sure you take all your things."

"We were just getting to know each other," she said.

Mitchell grabbed the woman by the hair. "Get the hell out! Now! I have some important phone calls to make."

42 Angered by Mitchell's tone, the woman was dressed within minutes. She left the suite and hurried to the car parked behind the building.

The driver helped her into the back seat. He put her bag into the trunk.

She shut the privacy glass and dialed her phone.

"We're clear," she said. "I left him alone in the suite. Is the bank transfer done?"

A voice on the other end gave her the answer she wanted to hear. "The confirmation is coming your way via text."

When she saw the number, her eyes widened. She had really hit the jackpot this time.

She tapped on the privacy glass. The driver slid it open.

"Where to, Ma'am?" he asked.

"The airport," the woman said. "I think it's time for an extended vacation someplace far away from here."

"Anyplace in particular you're looking forward to visiting?"

"The sky's the limit. I just came into more money than I could ever spend in my lifetime."

"Then the airport it is," the driver said as he pulled off.

Upstairs, Mitchell jumped into the shower, and then he dressed. Half an hour later, he called Sonny.

It was 11:45 p.m.

"Hey, man," he said. "I think I'm gonna' go into the office for a few hours tonight so I can catch up on some paperwork. Stop by the suite and make sure everything's cleaned up. I'm meeting the wife here tomorrow for lunch."

"Glad that you two are back on track. That's good," his lifelong friend said. "I'll head over there in a few and make sure it's ready for your romantic lunch."

"Thanks, man. Now that all the drama about those pictures is behind us, maybe we can start fresh. By the way, did you take care of those flowers?" Mitchell asked.

43

"I did. Delivered them to her myself. Yellow roses, right?"

"Yeah, her favorite. After the election, I've got to do something extra special for her. Maybe she'd like a cruise to the Mediterranean for just the two of us."

"She'd like that, man. And she deserves it for putting up with you through all this."

"You're right. Start looking into that for me. I'll touch base with you first thing in the morning about other campaign business."

Mitchell hung up the phone and made his way to the elevator. He hit the "L" button as he entered.

Twenty-seven floors later, the elevator stopped and the doors opened. Mitchell took one step towards them.

Suddenly, a gunshot rang out.

Mitchell fell against the wall and slid down to the floor with a thud.

"Special delivery," a vindicated voice said. A hand reached in and pushed the button to close the elevator doors. A single yellow rose fell next to Mitchell's body before the doors closed.

Mitchell tried to get up, but his legs didn't work. With help just an arm's reach away, his breathing became shallow and his eyelids suddenly felt as heavy as boulders. The doors quietly shut, leaving Mitchell to ponder his current predicament.

Suddenly becoming president didn't seem like the most important item on his "To Do" list.

"Help me," he slurred.

Unable to move, the last thing Mitchell remembered was hearing his grandfather's voice and the words from one of the old man's favorite sermons: "Pride goeth before destruction. And a haughty spirit before a fall."

As he lay gurgling in a pool of his own blood, the elevator began its slow climb to the penthouse level and Mitchell Rush drifted off into what he prayed would *not* be his final sleep.

44

DAY THREE
BEST LAID PLANS

Mitchell Rush is the Republican candidate for President of the United Sates in the 2012 election. Born in Memphis to a prosperous, upper class, family of judges, politicians, and lawyers, no one ever doubted that Mitchell would become a powerful U.S. Senator and future President. From infancy, he had been groomed and prepared for it. Politics was in his DNA and his passion kept his heart beating. He knew no other way to live his life. At this stage of his illustrious and influential career, the Presidency seemed to be his only viable option. He would surely die if he did not achieve his heart's desire.

Mitchell and number forty-four had some similarities. They shared August birthdates, ten years apart. Rush in 1951 and forty-four in 1961. They both attended Harvard Law School and served as President of the Harvard Law Review, though Mitchell served when forty-four was still a community organizer. Each taught constitutional law, Mitchell at John Marshall Law School in Chicago versus forty-four at the University of Chicago Law School. Both were African American Senators who wanted to "change" America. But unlike forty-four, he was a conservative Republican who had no wife or children.

It was close to 2:30 a.m. on a rather chilly Saturday. Mitchell felt unusually restless. He tossed and turned as he lay on his plush Stearns and Foster mattress located in the bedroom of his luxurious condominium on Water Street NW, #A-7, one of Georgetown's most prestigious addresses. He was anal when it came to cleanliness; therefore the condo was kept beyond immaculate. Nothing appeared to be out of place. Paintings and knick knacks were minimal. He loved the color white and believed it made him feel closer to God. Ninety-eight percent of the furniture, the walls, and carpet were white. Splashes of red, his power color, were used as an accent. His house provided a haven, a sanctuary where simplicity was the key to his peace of mind. He didn't have many close friends, just associates, but he preferred it that way. Long ago he had decided that fewer contemporaries were definitely best and unwarranted drama never fit well in his political agenda. Mitchell, a mover and a shaker, the "go-to-guy" if you needed to raise money or a bill passed.

The expensive campaign had begun to wind down. Only a week away, Mitchell was concerned about the election. He had tried every ethical and unethical tactic to gain an advantage but to no avail, he kept coming in second in the polls and at least ten points behind in each of the four key battleground states, Pennsylvania, Virginia, Florida and Ohio. If his numbers didn't go up in these states soon, he might as well concede now. For the first time in his career, frustration, despair, discouragement, and fright plagued his thoughts. *How could this be? I've done everything. I've crossed every "t" and dotted every "i".*

The past few weeks left him exhausted from the grueling campaign, the debates, and all of the nonstop fundraising events that he had attended. If he had to kiss or take a picture with one more snot-nose kid or crying baby he would choke somebody! Sleep, these days, seemed insignificant. It had only been a few hours since he was online perusing the New York Times Best

Seller's list and deciding if he was going to purchase James Patterson's latest novel 'Cross' while he listened to Leno deliver his infamous one-liner jokes on his sprawling seventy-two inch LCD television.

Unaware that he had drifted off to sleep, Mitchell dreamt it was finally Inauguration Day and he stood proudly at the podium. Seven inches of snow blanketed D.C. the night before and the temperature had dropped to eighteen degrees, but hundreds of thousands of people braved frostbitten extremities to see him sworn in. The vibrant, blue sky and clouds were breathtaking. His heart palpitated at an unfamiliar rate. He hoped he wouldn't drop dead before he completed his oath. Finally, it had come to this glorious day. A lifetime of hard work and dedication of perfecting his craft was about to pay off with the highest honor, President of the United States of America.

Even though forty-four would be known as a one term President, the crowd was still ecstatic. They roared with excitement. Why wouldn't they be full of pride? Another well-qualified African American had risen to the top and had achieved what others deemed impossible. America stood still and witnessed again a historical event as the forty-fifth President of the USA took his oath.

The distinguished Supreme Court Chief Justice Duke R. Welsh was about to administer the Oath of Office. The crowd was cheering and chanting Mitchell's name. He waved to his constituents as he placed his right hand on the bible. It was the same 1861 bible from Abraham Lincoln's inauguration that his predecessor used. Oh...how he wished his parents and grandparents were alive to see this momentous moment. The Rush legacy would be elevated to new heights as they kept pace with the Kennedys in wealth, power, and stature. Indeed, it was a day of celebration. Yes, forty-four may have been the first, but he could claim to be the first who had substantial clout and an aristocratic lineage. There would be no celebrities or news reporters lurking around his past trying to dig up dirt regarding his citizenship, educational background and his qualifications. He was the real deal and very proud to be an American.

Mitchell was beaming and overjoyed with excitement. He raised his left land hand to begin his oath. Suddenly, the bible opened up and began to yank his body into the book. He tried to pull away, but the force that gripped him was beyond any strength he could muster to jerk away. Chief Justice Welsh's face became distorted as it transformed into the burly Silas Luxapher. Mitchell horrified at the horrendous scene, which was unfolding, looked out into the open forum and watched the crowd turn into unrecognizable Zombie-like human beings.

Mitchell tried to scream, but his vocal cords were strangled. He abruptly awakened from the shocking dream and found himself drenched in a cold sweat which saturated his blue satin pajamas and soaked his linens. He felt his blood pressure rise. His breathing became erratic and he tried to calm himself down. Shaken and discombobulated, he fumbled in the darkened room and reached for his smartphone from the mahogany nightstand. He quickly dialed a familiar number and prayed the call would be answered.

"I need to see you. Meet me in an hour at the southeast side of the MLK Memorial."

Mitchell quickly showered, dressed, grabbed his keys and smartphone, and walked out the door. He was met by Secret Service Agent Max Donnelly. Agent Donnelly, a decorated war veteran who took his job very seriously, had thirty-five years of loyal service in protecting Presidential candidates and Presidents.

"Senator, where are you going?" Agent Donnelly sternly asked.

"Calm down, Agent." Mitchell said and patted him on the back. "I will be back in a couple of hours. I need to take care of some personal business." Mitchell kept walking toward the elevator.

Agent Donnelly swiftly followed Mitchell. "Sir, I can't let you go out by yourself, especially at this time of night. It's too dangerous."

48

The elevator doors opened and Mitchell stepped in with Agent Donnelly on his heels. All of a sudden, Mitchell pushed Donnelly back out of the elevator doors. "I said no protection!"

"But Sir, I have to follow protocol."

"Tonight, Agent, there is no protocol. I assure you, I will be back. I know you are close to retirement and have devoted your life to serving your country, but if you insist on following me you will regret it. Do you want to lose your pension and be a disgrace to your family?"

"No, Sir, I don't want to be unemployed, but it's my job to protect you. I would never forgive myself if something happened to you. Please sir, let me come with you. I promise you won't know I am there."

Agent Donnelly again tried to approach him and Rush forcibly pushed back.

Mitchell angrily raised his voice. "If you follow me, I assure you, I will have you fired before the sun rises! Do you understand me?"

49

Begrudgingly, Agent Donnelly raised his hands in defeat, relinquished his pursuit and watched the elevators doors close.

The night was slightly frigid, but not yet freezing. The stars were unusually bright. A colder winter was defiantly around the corner. The cherry blossoms were now bare and the anticipation of the first snowfall filled the air.

The white granite MLK statue was situated on four acres, located at West Potomac Park in Washington, D.C., southwest of the Washington Mall. The official address of the statue was 1964 Independence Avenue, S.W. which commemorated the year the Civil Rights Act of 1964 became law. The statue was the perfect meeting place for Mitchell because it gave him hope that one day a similar massive structure would be erected in his honor.

Mitchell arrived at the statue, but his invited guess was nowhere to be found. Impatiently, he checked his watch. Only fifty minutes had passed since he placed his urgent call. Out of the dark he heard a familiar voice.

"Mitchell, are you here?"

Mitchell walked toward the gentle voice. "I'm over here."

Tina Hillsdale walked out of the shadows. The moonlight cast a soft illumination on the unbelievably radiant, stately, and beautiful woman. Even at this ungodly time of night she still made Mitchell's soul vibrate with happiness. It was an undeniable happiness he never felt for any other woman. She had all the qualities he ever wanted in a partner, in a potential wife. She graduated, Summa Cum Laude from Yale University with a PhD in Financial Economics. She was well versed, spoke seven languages, beyond sexy, driven, confident, traveled around the world, and most importantly she held the title of forty-four's Chief of Staff.

50 They had met back in Memphis during their sophomore year in high school when her father, Poindexter Hillsdale accepted a position at his grandfather's firm, Ronald Rush Esquire and Associates. Her father quickly became one of his grandfather's prodigies, while Tina and Mitchell became fast friends and eventually lovers. Even when they went their separate ways in college, Mitchell kept track of Tina and he would make a point of seeing her at least twice, sometimes four times a year. Whenever they met old feelings and desires loomed in the air just like they were teenagers discovering each other for the very first time. Both of them had endured their tribulations, but they had an unbreakable, uncanny bond which Mitchell counted on to obtain the information he needed from Tina. She held the key to his success.

Tina appeared annoyed at her longtime friend. "Mitchell, what the heck are you doing? What could you possibly want from me in the middle of the night?"

Mitchell walked closer to Tina and grabbed her hand. "I needed to see you. I...I need to ask you a favor."

"Seriously, Mitchell, a favor and it couldn't wait until morning?"

"You look beautiful under the starlight and you smell incredible. Is that Dior?" Mitchell asked as he leaned in to kiss Tina.

Tina waved her hand in Mitchell's face. "Back off, Mitchell, you know I am engaged!"

"Yes, I know, engaged to the smug Congressman, James Russell. I'll never know what you see in him. And yet, here you are in the middle of the night with me. Tell me Tina, where is your knight?"

"He's in Pittsburgh visiting his ailing grandmother. You know he's a lot like you, arrogant, pompous, and self-righteous."

Mitchell snickered and rubbed his goatee. "Is that right? Come on and kiss me for old time sake. I can look in your eyes and see you want me. Even through that lovely designer wool coat, I can feel the heat coming off of your body. The essence of your womanhood permeates the air. Your soul cannot betray your heart. Why don't we go back to my apartment where we can get comfortable? I'll draw you a nice warm bubble bath, fix your favorite Cinnamon tea with a spoonful of honey, massage your tense neck, then we can make love and have some political pillow talk? Don't you recall how you used to enjoy our romps so much? Surely you remember my dear, how I made your toes curl as you hollered my name? We used to make love for hours at a time and sometimes we would barricade ourselves in my home for an entire weekend. Aw...sweet, sweet, sweet memories are all I have some nights to get me through. How about you, can you remember?"

51

Tina's dazzling hazel eyes sparkled, just like Mitchell anticipated. Everything was going as planned. Convinced he had struck a nerve, he knew she would soon comply. He was the master manipulator and he knew all the right buttons to push to ignite Tina's sexual hot spots. He moved closer and closed the gap between them. The wind started to stir and blew Tina's long, loosely curled, brunette hair all over her face. Mitchell repositioned the hair which had blown in her eyes and gently caressed her cheek. Hesitantly, she moved his hand and took a few steps back to escape the unexpected desire that started to burn within.

"Mitchell, I really can't play these games with you. We are not love-struck teenagers anymore. If you don't tell me what you want I am leaving!"

"Okay, okay, there is no need to be hostile. Well...it's about your job."

"You need to speak to me about my job? Mitchell, you know I can't speak to you about anything which pertains to my position. You, of all people, know what goes on in the Oval Office is strictly confidential."

"Tina, please hear me out before you respond. Can you do that for me?"

Reluctantly, she agreed, "Go ahead, Mitchell, but you've been warned. The answer will still be no!"

Mitchell smiled at his impatient ex-lover. She was so cute and feisty. "Being Chief of Staff allows you access to privileged information, like the President's foreign policy, etc. I am sure you have been following the election closely. As you know, I am behind in the polls. I must have an edge. I need something that will turn this election on its heels. The last debate is on Wednesday and I need a knockout if I plan to win. I want you to copy all of forty-four's files by Friday night. We will meet here around the same time. There has to be something I can use against him."

"What? Are you kidding me? Are you trying to punk me? This has to be some sick twisted joke! I can't do that, Mitchell! I won't commit political suicide, not for you, not for anyone! I have worked too hard for my career. I can't believe you have the audacity to ask me to compromise my job, my livelihood...for you. You are crazy, Mitchell Rush! I thought I knew you, but this is a new low. I don't even recognize you!"

Tina turned and began to walk away. Mitchell snatched her arm and jerked her toward him. They stood nose to nose. Mitchell growled with displeasure as his manhood grew with pleasure. He loved the chase and loved to be a conqueror. He wanted to ravage her right then and there. He felt her heart beating rapidly. Her body wanted to yield to the carnal tension. Mitchell softly caressed her lips with his; a light moan escaped their slightly ajar mouths.

"You will get me those documents or I will tell everyone how your beloved Congressman's family is importing blood diamonds into the US and selling them all across the world."

Tina furiously wiped her mouth. She raised her voice several octaves and spewed spittle at Mitchell, "You don't have any proof!"

"I don't? Try me! We can start by referencing the oversized pear-shaped diamond ring you have on your pretty well-manicured hand. It appears to be at least twelve karats. Correct?"

Tina ignored his allegation and plunged her hand into her coat pocket.

"Tell me Mitchell, has your career really come down to this? Blackmailing the woman you claim you have loved your entire life? Making false accusations against people who have never harmed you, really?"

"Is it indeed a false indictment? Come now, Tina, you are an intelligent woman. I know you must have your own suspicions. You know your precious Congressman lives a luxurious lifestyle which is way beyond his current salary. What makes him any better than me? You seem to enjoy sleeping with men who have a dark side."

Tina slapped Mitchell across the face.

Momentarily stunned, he looked toward the ground. He couldn't bear to see the hurt in Tina's eyes. He guessed he deserved his punishment, but he had to do what he had to do, even if it meant hurting his one true love. He regained his composure.

"Look Tina, I don't want to hurt you. I have come too far to turn back now. As the great Malcolm X, proclaimed 'by any means necessary'. You, my darling, are the means to my end.

Come over to the right side, resign as Chief of Staff, turn away from the Democratic Party and marry me. Become the First Lady of the United States. You will run circles around the treasured Michelle. Becoming a Rush will give you more prestige and power than you could ever imagine. You will be a part of a dynasty which has lasted generations. We both know your Congressman doesn't have the fortitude to hold such an esteem position. He will never become President. Besides, he is twenty years younger than you. How long do you honestly think your beauty will last? One day it's going to fade. You know he is going to want a child, something you can never give him and then sadly my dear, dear Tina, the good Congressman will be out the door."

Tears streamed down Tina's face. She screamed at Mitchell. "I am appalled by you, Mitchell Rush! I never thought in a million years I would hate you!"

Mitchell chuckled and simply replied, "Nonsense."

Tina raised her hand to slap him again. Mitchell clutched her wrist, pulled her closer and forcibly kissed her.

This time Tina did not reject his advances. Instead, she embraced him with every fiber of her being. Her body had yearned many nights for his touch. She felt alive again and tingled with electrical impulses. In her six year relationship with James, she never felt this sensation with him. When she and James made love she often closed her eyes and had flashbacks of her time with Mitchell. She had loved Mitchell from the first day she met him so many years ago...a lifetime ago.

Tina tried to live righteously. She was committed to James. What she and Mitchell had was a thing of the past. Finally, her conscience caught up with her desires. She disengaged their dancing entwined tongues. "I'll see what I can do," were the last words Tina spoke as she drifted into the darkness, leaving Mitchell behind, alone with all his mischievous feelings.

Feeling exceptionally confident that his mission had been accomplished, Mitchell jogged back to his parked Range Rover. Once inside his vehicle, he caught his breath and wiped the perspiration from his forehead. He closed his eyes and leaned against the headrest as he replayed visions of Tina and their kiss. He hadn't realized how much he missed her. Not marrying her turned out to be the one true regret of his life. He ached to caress every inch of her body again, to have her perfume linger on his sheets and in his condo long after she had gone. Obsessed by his memories, he escaped to a simpler time when love was pure and all consuming. A smile formed across his face. "One day, my darling, I shall have you again."

"You had an interesting night." A raspy voice echoed from the backseat of the car.

Mitchell jumped. "What the hell?"

A startled and shaken Mitchell looked in his rearview mirror. "How did you get in here? How did you know where I was? Are you following me, Silas?"

"Mitchell, don't let your paranoia overtake you. I just happened to be in the neighborhood and saw your vehicle. It's not like you parked in an inconspicuous spot. I'm surprised TMZ or Entertainment Tonight didn't film you and Ms. Hillsdale's little tryst. I must say Mitchell, you have good taste. She is a beauty."

Irritated, Mitchell spoke. "Silas, it's late. Cut to the chase. What do you want?"

It had been a week since the six foot six Silas Luxapher arrived early in the morning at his door, bearing a gift; an antique book with seven rusty hinges. Silas proceeded to tell him he could use one or a combination of the tools in the book to help him accomplish his goals. But he only had seven days to achieve them. Time was ticking away.

Silas leaned forward from the backseat. His stale-smelling, hot breath grazed Mitchell's right ear and neck. "I don't want anything, Mitchell, but I do like the blood diamond scandal. Use the book!"

"How did...?" Mitchell asked, but just as quickly as he had appeared Silas vanished into the night.

Mitchell started the car and headed back home. He had a lot to think about. Executing his plan was crucial. There was no turning back.

Morning was fast approaching as he exited the elevator to his condo. A relieved Agent Donnelly nodded in his direction.

"Agent Donnelly, your shift was over a couple of hours ago," Mitchell informed him in a superior tone.

"Yes, Sir, it was, but I could not leave with a clear conscience knowing you had not come home. Is everything alright, Sir?"

"Yes, Agent, for the first time in a while I think everything is going to be okay. Go home, get some sleep, kiss your wife and play with your kids. You will be back here before you know it."

"Yes Sir, I think, I will. Good night...I mean have a good morning."

Mitchell smiled and walked into his condo. He threw his keys on the kitchen counter and headed toward his library to retrieve the book Silas Luxapher had given him. There it was, lying on his oversized antique cherry wood desk which once belonged to his great grandfather, Miles Rush. He remembered that, at the age of six or seven, he would sneak downstairs in the middle of the night and peek in the door of his brilliant grandfather's study and watch him write one of his many political dissertations. The desk seemed gigantic back then and felt as if it possessed some mythical, magical power. The heirloom became one of his most cherished possessions.

Mitchell walked behind the desk, pulled out the red leather chair, sat down and grabbed the book. He flipped through the pages and went to Day 2. He couldn't believe what he was reading. *To achieve is to believe. You must plan accordingly and win no matter what. What you desire is right at your fingertips. To activate your next steps and ensure your destiny is fulfilled you must cut your left ring finger. Then let your blood trickle into the spine of this book. Turn the spine red with your blood and whisper three times what it is you desire the most in this life. I want to be President. I want to be President. I want to be President!*

Mitchell dropped the book on the desk. He shook his head in disbelief and then rested it in the palm of his hands. He could not comprehend the words which popped out from the page. He picked the book back up and over the next few hours he re-examined the simple passage. He memorized every word and allowed it to resonate in his spirit.

He had to clear his mind before he lost it. He went into the kitchen and opened his favorite bottle of Beaujolais. He loved the fruity taste of the French wine. He gulped down the first glass and allowed himself to savor the second one. His mind raced. *Could a book with blood dripping down the spine possibly secure his win?* "Insane!" He shouted.

His cell phone rang and brought him back to reality. "Hello, this is Rush."

"Mitchell, it's me, Tina."

"Aw...Tina, it hasn't been that long since we gazed into each other's eyes. Do you miss me already?"

"Mitchell, listen to me. Since I left you I have been thinking about what you asked me. I know I told you I would see what I could do, but I can't do it. Never contact me again. Erase my number and the next time you see me it has to be strictly professional."

"Tina, I am not happy. I don't like to be denied. You know how I get when I have been crossed. You will not like the consequences of your actions. I urge you to reconsider your decision. Why don't you come over and we can talk about it. I just opened your favorite bottle of wine."

"Mitchell, what don't you understand? I don't want to come over, not now, not ever. As much as my heart is torn into pieces over losing my best friend, I have to let you go. I refuse to go down this self-destructive path with you. I wish you the best of luck. I sincerely hope you find true happiness. Goodbye, Mitchell."

An enraged Mitchell stared at the disconnected cell phone. "That bitch will regret the day she crossed Mitchell Rush!"

Mitchell poured another glass of wine and walked over to the twelve piece knife block set which was on top of the marble counter. "What do I have to lose?" He stated as he considered which knife he was going to use to spill his blood. He picked up the razor-sharp steak knife and caught his capsulated reflection in the gleaming silver of the blade. His bloodshot eyes looked back at him. Tina's words "I barely recognize you," quivered in his intoxicated ears.

Mitchell stumbled back toward the library and sat down. He pulled the knife from his pants pocket and grabbed the book. His hands shook uncontrollably as he brought the utensil to his left ring finger. He was about to strike his digit and stopped. His courage waned. Sweat formulated on his brow. His face began to flush as vomit crept up his throat. He swallowed. He opened the bottom desk drawer, grabbed a glass and the opened bottle of Hennessy. He poured the liquid courage and guzzled it. "I barely recognize you," taunted him.

For a split second his courage returned. It was now or never. Again he gripped the knife. This time he quickly struck his limb. "Jesus!" he yelled. He had cut too deep. Blood poured from his appendage and splattered onto his pants leg and shirt. He snatched the book and let the crimson substance stream down the spine. He shouted from the top of his lungs, "I want to be President! I want to be President! I want to be President!" He quickly exhaled, grabbed a handkerchief from his lapel, tied it around his finger, applied pressure and anxiously waited for the book to do something.

Unexpectedly, the lights in the room began to flicker off and on. The book rattled and bounced up and down on the desk. The bloodstained pages flipped back and forth. Silas Luxapher's exceptionally loud deranged laughter seemed to emanate from the Bose speakers and filled the room making the walls shudder. The desk, lamps and other office furniture began to tremble as the floor started to move. The door to the library furiously opened and closed. Mitchell was transfixed by the unfolding events as he sat paralyzed with fear. Luxapher's glee was unbearable. It played over and over again like a broken record. He covered his ears to shut out the boisterous voice. Why couldn't he see him? Mitchell thought he was dreaming again, but the pain from his still bleeding, almost severed finger was all too real.

It seemed like hours had passed, but it had only been a few moments. All at once the strange occurrences stopped. Mitchell gauged the entire room. Everything was in place like nothing ever happened. He looked down at the book which had turned to the passage of Day 2. At the bottom of the page he witnessed with unbelieving eyes, his blood being used like ink as it mysteriously transcribed *Mitchell Rush, President of the United States of America. Signed, sealed and delivered.* Mitchell blacked out.

Mitchell was awakened from his short-lived induced drunken slumber by the loud banging coming from his front door. "Senator Rush, open the door! Senator Rush, I need you to open the door!" Agent Donnelly repeatedly shouted.

Mitchell was disoriented. He felt like he had been hit over the head with a brick. He looked down at his finger and was disturbed at the overly drenched bloody handkerchief. The throbbing from his finger was excruciating and the pain had engulfed his entire hand. The banging at the front door continued.

Agent Donnelly screamed, "Senator, if you don't open the door. I am coming in!"

Mitchell got his bearings. "I'm coming," he shrieked as he walked toward the door.

When he unlocked the door, he was met by two Sig Sauer P229s; .357 caliber pistols in his face. Agent Donnelly and Agent West had drawn their guns.

"Agents, please lower your weapons. Why are they drawn? You already know I am the only one here."

Agent Donnelly and Agent West had perplexed looks on their faces and lowered their weapons. Agent Donnelly looked at the disheveled and blood-stained Senator. He pointed at Agent West indicating he should search the premises and gently moved the Senator into the hallway.

"Senator, we heard loud screaming. I was about to break down the door. Sir, what happened? You are bleeding. I am going to call medical."

Still gathering his wits, Mitchell tried to come up with a logical explanation. "Uh...Agent Donnelly, I thank you for coming to my rescue, but there is nothing wrong. The screams you heard were a horror movie I was watching. I must have drifted off to sleep and hadn't realized the volume was up."

"Sir, how do you explain all the blood on your clothing?"

Before he could answer Agent West appeared in the hallway. "All clear, Sir."

"Thank you, Agent West." Agent Donnelly finally holstered his gun and led Mitchell back inside the foyer of the condo while Agent West stayed posted outside the front door.

Mitchell's mind struggled for clarity as he looked down at his injury. Agent Donnelly was relentless in his pursuit of answers.

"Sir, I need to know about the blood."

"Agent Donnelly, I don't understand why I am being interrogated. It's really no big deal. I got hungry. I was making a steak, dicing some mushrooms and onions when I cut myself. Apparently, I drank too much wine. That's all, a simple accident."

Agent Donnelly could smell Mitchell's disgusting breath a mile away. He could confirm that part of his statement was accurate. Agent Donnelly surveyed the kitchen area and didn't notice a steak, dirty dishes or any blood stains. The kitchen was spotless. There was no conclusive evidence that Mitchell had been preparing a meal. Unconvinced that the Senator was being truthful, he did know there was no one else in the residence.

Perhaps, it was just a horror movie and an accident. Mitchell could tell Agent Donnelly was contemplating his story and wasn't yet convinced of its truthfulness.

"Senator, judging by the blood saturating your clothing and the rag or whatever you used as a tourniquet, it appears you have a serious injury. I can tell you did not nick your finger. Let me call a doctor to look at your hand. I believe you probably need several stitches and to be honest Sir, you don't look well."

Mitchell walked up to Agent Donnelly and used his uninjured hand to shake the agent's hand as he ushered him to the front door. "Agent Donnelly, I truly appreciate your concern about my well-being, but a doctor won't be necessary. Now, if you don't mind, I need to get back to working on my acceptance speech. If there is nothing else you need to check on, I really must go."

Agent Donnelly couldn't hide his concern. The Senator had exhibited strange behavior in recent days. "No, Senator, there is nothing else. I'll let you get back to your work. I'll be right here you if need me for anything, anything at all."

61

"Thank you, Agent. I will keep that in mind. I promise next time I'll order take out."

Agent Donnelly finally left. Mitchell ran back to his library and opened the book. Perhaps it had all been a hallucination. Bipolar did run on his mother's side of the family. Maybe, the stress of the campaign had triggered an episode, but he wasn't dreaming, hallucinating or crazy because the blood-stained book with his name written in it was right where he had left it. Mitchell went to the bathroom, opened the medicine cabinet and found a bottle of almost expired Tylenol with codeine. He popped two pills, quickly downed a glass of water and headed back toward the library. He flipped open his laptop and started executing his plan.

It was close to midnight on Sunday. Mitchell worked nonstop and had not taken a break. His plan was coming together. He was amazed at the phenomenal knowledge he had unexpectedly obtained about blood diamonds. The book had given him more than he could ever explain and accelerated his

IQ on the subject. The more he wrote, the more his plan came together. Documents and facts appeared out of nowhere. At times it was like his computer was typing by itself. He now possessed real power which resonated deep down in his soul. He had been taken to another realm and was now all-knowing. Yes, the book changed his life.

By Friday morning when he scheduled his press conference, forty-four would be in hot water and the good Congressman would be in deep trouble. The election would be turned upside down. Congressional hearings would immediately take place and he would be the triumphant hero for discovering the deceitful scandal. America loved a champion and they would repay him by electing him President. His plan was fool proof.

His cell phone rang. Mitchell looked at the number and wasn't at all surprised by the caller's identity. He knew she would come around.

"Tina, my dear, I thought I would never hear from you again. What do you want?"

"Mitchell, meet me at our usual spot and come alone. I'll be there in twenty minutes."

"I'll be there."

Mitchell grabbed his keys and walked out the door. Agent Donnelly stood there as usual.

"Senator, where are you going?"

"I'll be back, Agent. No security!"

"But Sir..."

"Agent, do I need to remind you about what I can do to your career?"

"No, Sir, I don't need a reminder."

"Good! Then we have an understanding?"

"I clearly, unequivocally, understand, Sir."

"I'll be back in a couple of hours." Mitchell informed him as he entered the elevator and closed the doors again in a defeated Agent Donnelly's face.

Mitchell made it to the MLK memorial in record time. He got out of his car and trudged through the snow toward the meeting place. Winter had quickly descended and it felt incredibly cold. As he approached the statute, he could see Tina all bundled up and holding what appeared to be a couple of boxes.

"Tina, it's good to see you."

"What happened to your hand?"

"Oh...just a slight battle with a steak knife and I lost."

"You should have a doctor look at it."

"Your concern is endearing. My Lord, you look good."

"Mitchell, I don't have time for your banter. I had to go to the office today. I got you what I could, but you have to promise to shred everything. I want you to understand this is a one-time deal. I never want to hear you say anything about this or speak about those blood diamonds again."

"I knew you would come around, my love, and see things my way. You never could say no to me."

"I don't see things your way. Your vision is cloudy. You have no ethical compass. I don't know what happened to you during the course of this campaign, but you have lost your way. Besides, I didn't do it for you, Mitchell."

"You didn't?"

"No, I did it for James. I love him, Mitchell. I truly love him. I have waited a long time to fall in love again. I could not sit back and watch you destroy him. He is a good man and doesn't deserve your unjustified wrath."

"Whatever Tina, you are in denial. You will always love me."

"You are right. I will always love you, Mitchell. I will always love the man you used to be. The man who stands in front of me today would not lust over or envy something someone else had, even if it is the Presidency. You have left a legacy which will live on in history books for generations to come. You have done great things for our country and that should be enough. Instead you have allowed yourself to become consumed by this election and the idea of becoming President. I can't love you anymore. It's time to let you go. I am going to move on with my present life and that life is with James."

Tina handed Mitchell the boxes and walked away.

Mitchell was jubilant. He could use forty-four's documents against him and still execute his blood diamond scandal. He couldn't believe his good fortune. Tina would be pissed about his impending plans and certainly would never speak to him again, but in times of war and fighting the final battle there was always collateral damage. Of course, in years to come, he would give the Congressman and forty-four a Presidential pardon. All would be forgiven and time would heal all wounds.

Mitchell exited the elevator doors and Agent Donnelly instinctively grabbed the boxes from him.

"No!" Mitchell bellowed as he snatched the boxes back from Agent Donnelly. He grimaced with pain as a heavy carton hit his finger.

Agent Donnelly was taken aback. "Sir, please let me help you."

"Just open the damn door and move out of my way."

Agent Donnelly complied. Mitchell pushed past him and slammed the door in the Agent's face. He quickly threw the contents of the containers on the living room floor. He ran to the bathroom, retrieved two more codeine pills, downed them with some water and quickly retreated to the living room.

Friday night had descended. Mitchell lost track of time while reading all of the documents Tina had given him over and over again. "Useless! Absolutely, useless," he concluded. Forty-four was on the level. Despite popular belief, his foreign policy was air tight. Everything forty-four had done in his administration was above board. Mitchell could not find a blemish on forty-four's record and was beyond pissed.

"It's okay. It's okay. I can still implicate him with the Congressman," he said, trying to convince himself. He headed back to the library and printed off the documents he prepared for tomorrow's press conference. Mitchell had now been up for seventy-two hours. He had not shaved, bathed or eaten since Saturday, but now he needed to get it together and look his best as he delivered the earth-shattering news to the country. Yes, tomorrow would be the first day of new chapter of his life. President Rush sounded so good.

The Today Show blared from the television. It was 7:30 a.m. Friday morning and the press conference was scheduled for ten. Mitchell had finally showered, shaved and eaten a hardy breakfast of poached eggs, three strips of bacon, and two slices of wheat toast with strawberry jam. He washed it all down with a cup of piping hot, black coffee.

65

He loaded the dishwasher and headed toward the bedroom to get dressed. Mitchell entered his large closet and retrieved the newly-purchased navy blue pinstriped Armani double- breasted suit. He snatched the lightly starched white shirt off the rack and pulled out a red tie which he thought was an excellent choice. His indigo Stacy Adams were buffed and polished. He had to admit that, for an older gentleman, he was a dashing, good-looking man. He still worked out and maintained his physique. His six-pack was slightly fading, but overall he looked and felt better than some men half his age.

Wow! Lights, camera, action! Mitchell was ready to meet the media. He felt calm, confident and ready to start the extraordinary day.

He was enthusiastic as he watched the news report which stated he was gaining momentum in the polls. Mitchell had actually pulled ahead in Florida and had a slight lead in Ohio. He felt assured that a victory was on the horizon.

The house phone distracted Mitchell's morning routine.

"Rush, speaking."

"Mitchell, my boy, today's a big day for you. Are you ready?"

"Silas, why are you calling?"

"I wanted to check on you. I am so pleased you finally grew some balls and used the book. How is your finger?"

"Silas, do you have my place under surveillance?"

"Come now, Mitchell that would be highly illegal. You have a great press conference and congratulations. I smell a prestigious position in my future."

"What? What prestigious position? What are you talking about, Silas? You don't have a political background. To be honest I really don't know what you do."

"You would be correct, Mr. President, I don't have any political qualifications, but in spite of my lack of credentials you will make the appointment happen. In fact, I want to be your Chief of Staff."

66

Mitchell roared with astonishment. "Silas, you need to go back to sleep and start your morning over. Surely sleep deprivation has made you delusional. There is no way in hell that is going to happen."

"But Mitchell, are you sure you haven't already been to hell? Read the fine print in the book. Once you have activated it and put your heart desires in motion, you must oblige the person who bestowed the book to you. Anything I ask cannot and will not be denied."

Mitchell hung up the phone without responding to Silas's outrageous request. He grabbed the book from the coffee table and turned to the last page. It confirmed that he would never be out of the clutches of Silas Luxapher. What had he done? Had he made a deal with the devil? He felt a migraine coming on and quickly swallowed the last of his pain pills.

It was exactly 9:55 a.m. when Mitchell and his entourage arrived at the Fairmont Washington Hotel. At 10:00 a.m. Mitchell approached the podium. Several dozen reporters had gathered for the event. They were scurrying to their seats and ensuring all their microphones and recording devices were working in optimal condition. They could not afford to miss any of this breaking news, even though none of them had an inkling of what would unfold.

Mitchell cleared his throat before he spoke. "Good morning, everyone. I appreciate all of you showing up on such short notice. I will not be taking any questions. At the end of the conference when you exit, you will receive a package I have prepared for your review.

"As you know, conflict or blood diamonds as they are often called, are mined in a war zone and are sold to finance insurgents and invading army's war efforts. African miners are employed to get these diamonds and are exposed to dreadful living conditions and even worse working conditions.

"Blood diamonds have contributed to devastating conflicts in countries such as Angola, Cote d'Ivoire, the Democratic Republic of Congo and Sierra Leone. About two-thirds of the world's diamonds are extracted from Africa. It has been estimated that blood diamonds represent four percent of the total trade in rough diamonds. Others estimate blood diamonds have amounted to as much as fifteen percent of the total diamond trade.

67

"The United Nations Security Council Resolution 1173 and 1176 bans the sale of these blood diamonds from Angola. Per the World Diamond Council, these resolutions have subdued the illegal diamond trade which has declined to approximately one percent and has remained at this percentage since 2004. However, the 2000 Fowler Report investigated and found countries, organizations and individuals who are still involved in this trade. This report clearly linked diamonds to third world conflicts which led to the United Nations Security Council Resolution 1295, as well as the Kimberly Process Certification Scheme (KPCS), established in 2003.

"I have been following the KPCS for at least nine years and I have gathered intelligence that this program does not guarantee that the diamonds which are being traded are one hundred percent conflict free. I have investigated beyond the Fowler Report regarding American companies who have been secretly importing these blood diamonds into the United States and are selling them to unknowing American citizens.

"You will find the 2012 Rush Report outlines specific details of these people who want to continue to disobey the laws of this country for their own selfish financial gain. The report is shocking in particular when our leaders are exposed. I am saddened to report that Congressman James Russell's family, who has been in the diamond exporting business for over eighty years, has participated and is still engaged in the business of blood diamond trading. I have proof in the documents I have prepared for you. The Congressman and his family have been illegally funding these insurgents. Also, the Congressman's family has been giving the President's step-grandmother, who lives in Kenya, and other members of his "African" family money directly from the sale of these diamonds. There is a complete listing of all the off shore accounts and other pertinent information to substantiate my findings. To go over everything in the report at this time would not be feasible. Please read the report for yourself. I am sure your conclusion will be that our current President cannot be allowed to continue to run and ruin this country while trying to support his other family who are not even American citizens. Congressman Russell must immediately take a leave of absence upon a full Congressional investigation."

The audience of reporters began to rumble amongst themselves as they tried to digest the shocking allegations. The news conference exploded into a frenzied scene. Reporters shouted at Mitchell. Hands were frantically raised and waving rapidly in hopes of asking him some questions. Mitchell surveyed the chaotic scene unfolding in front of him. He was very pleased with the outcome. He decided to end the conference.

"Ladies and gentlemen, calm down. As I stated before I am not taking any questions. Please pick up your briefing package on your way out. Thanks again. I appreciate you."

"Senator Rush, Senator, Senator!" Reporters shrieked as Mitchell excited the conference room.

Mitchell returned to his sanctuary and watched the news reports. CNN, Fox News, NBC and news outlets all around the world were talking about the great Mitchell Rush. The mind-blowing fallout for the Congressman and the President resulted in Mitchell's numbers in the polls increasing in all the battleground states. Forty-four cancelled the last debate. Tina was blowing up his phone with all sorts of irate messages. Reporters were camped outside of his condo, just waiting for him to make another statement. Time Magazine and every major news outlet were trying to contact him. His dream was only days away. He never imagined victory could taste so sweet.

For the first time in weeks, Mitchell slept the entire night, without dreams or nightmares. In fact, he slept for twenty-four hours straight. His peace of mind had returned.

Election eve was finally here. Mitchell sat at his dinner table, already celebrating his victory. His lobster was cooked to perfection. The garlic mashed potatoes and the asparagus were simply delicious. Tomorrow he would get up early, vote, then sit back and watch America make their choice.

69

Secluded in his condo since the news conference, Mitchell enjoyed these final days. He watched movies and finally finished reading "Cross". He did not have a care in the world and was thrilled he had used the power of the book. The scandal took on a life of its own, leaving an earthquake of destruction behind. He hadn't gotten any messages from Silas or Tina in a couple of days. A few persistent reporters still hounded him on a daily basis.

It was 1:30 a.m., the morning of Election Day. Mitchell had not gone to bed. He was still up watching and enjoying all of the news anchors who interjected their supposedly unbiased opinions. His cell phone rang.

"Tina, my dear, are you calling to tell me you reconsidered my offer to become First Lady? I knew you would change your mind once you saw I was a shoo-in, everyone, always wants to be on a winning team."

"Mitchell, can you meet me at the memorial?" Tina asked, her voice quivering.

"Sure. Tina, what's wrong? You sound upset."

"Um...there's nothing wrong. I just need to see you."

"Well, come over. I'm still at the same address."

"No, too many reporters are parked outside your house and you know the Secret Service is around."

"Okay...I get it. I'll see you in about thirty minutes. Are you sure there is nothing wrong?"

"I'm sure. I will see you then."

Mitchell felt a bit uneasy about meeting Tina. Perhaps, he should allow Agent Donnelly to tag along? No...Tina was trustworthy. She had proven her loyalty by getting forty-four's documents.

Mitchell exited his condo and saw Agent Donnelly posted by the elevator. He was not in the mood for his annoying, persistent questioning. Agent Donnelly pushed the elevator button for him and nodded. "Sir, what time should I expect your return?"

"Two hours tops. I have a big day today."

"Yes, Sir, you do. It's been an honor to serve you."

"Thank you. You are a respectable, hardworking man. I like you, Agent Donnelly."

Agent Donnelly was stunned. Mitchell stepped onto the elevator and the doors closed.

Mitchell had a different pep in his step as he approached the MLK statue. This time he was walking as the future President-Elect. Nothing or no one was going to ruin this day.

There she was; the love of his life looking breathtaking as always. He was determined to make Tina his wife before Inauguration Day. He needed her to complete his destiny. He didn't want to go down in history like his predecessor James Buchanan and be the second President who was not married while serving in office. Of course there were others, Jefferson,

Jackson, Van Buren and Arthur, but they didn't count because they were widowers.

Tina spoke first. "Mitchell, how could you? Tell me how you could go back on your word and go after James? I risked my career by giving you the files and you betrayed me."

"Those files were useless, Tina. Forty-four was more intelligent than I had predicted. I did what I felt was best for my career and my country. Forty-four having a second term was not in the cards. I had to ensure I was the one standing at the podium on January 21, 2013. Ironic isn't it? It's the same day we will celebrate ole Martin's birthday. Oh...I love it when a plan comes together. As I recall, I never gave you a direct answer regarding your James' future."

"How can you be so nonchalant? You have ruined James' career and shattered his family's business. We are talking about eight decades worth of work."

"I don't know what to say, Tina, except now you can leave James. The role of First Lady is beckoning you. Listen, can't you hear? It's whispering in the wind, First Lady Tina Rush. Doesn't it excite you?"

"You have sold your soul to the devil! I will never! Do you hear me, Mitchell? I will never marry you!"

The wind started to howl and blow at a furious rate. "So here he is the great Mitchell Rush in all his splendor and glory."

Tina and Mitchell jumped at the unfamiliar voice coming out the dark shadows of the night.

"Who are you? Show yourself," Mitchell shouted as he stepped in front of Tina to protect her.

The salt and pepper-haired Congressman James Russell, dressed in all black, appeared out of the darkness. Tina moved from behind Mitchell and approached James.

"James, how did you find me?"

"Perhaps you've heard of GPS?"

"Oh..."

"I knew you still loved him. Every time he came on the television, no matter what you were doing, no matter what time of day or night it was, you stopped to hear your one true love. Tell me Tina, did you really love me or was I just something to pass away the time until you left me to become First Lady?"

"James, what are you talking about? You know I love you. We are getting married in six months."

"I don't think so," James shouted at Tina.

Mitchell quietly stood still as the real life drama unfolded. He had initiated the last part of his plan and it was working out splendidly. He would be there to pick-up Tina's broken heart and then he would have her as his wife.

"James, I...I don't know what's come over you."

"I'll tell you. This evening I was at Capitol Hill and my secretary found me. She said she received this unmarked envelope with a note attached to it stating it was urgent and for my eyes only. Here take a look."

James threw the envelope at Tina. A wide grin spread across Mitchell's face.

Tina nervously opened the envelope. She had no idea what it contained.

A shrill echoed throughout the Washington Mall. "No!" Tina shouted from the top of her lungs. "James, I am so sorry." She apologized as the pictures of her and Mitchell fell on the snow-covered ground. She tried to embrace James, but he tossed her aside.

"Don't ever touch me again! Tell me Tina, are you the one who fed Mitchell all that crap about me and my family. Did you help him devise his elaborate lie? How long has this torrid affair been going on?"

Tina was crying uncontrollably. "James, you have to trust me. There is no affair. It was just a little kiss. I got caught up in old memories but, it didn't go any further. You have to trust me."

"Trust you? You want me to trust you? How can I ever trust you again when you are the one who has been sneaking out all hours of the night to meet him? You should have looked at all of the other pictures. You disgust me!"

"Please, James, I love you. We can work this out."

"Don't placate me. I have sacrificed everything for you. My family has been against this wedding and you from the first day I introduce you to them at the Fourth of July barbeque six years ago. A million times they've told me you are too old and I'll never have an heir. I defended you. I told them you were the best thing that ever happened to me and that we could adopt. A biological child did not define my love for you. They warned me time and time again. I told them no worries; we were going to have the perfect life. We planned to travel the world, build our dream home and live happily ever after. I feel like a fool! Who believes in a happy ending anyway?"

Tina continued to weep. Mitchell walked over and tried to console her. He was met by James' fist as it connected to the left side of his jaw. Stunned, Mitchell wiped the blood from the corner of his mouth.

73

"So, James, do you really want to travel down this road? I am going to give you one opportunity to turn back now. You better take a moment to think about this because once I start it's not going to be finished by you."

"Bring it, old man," a cocky James challenged.

Mitchell landed a punch on James' nose and broke it, but he almost passed out from the pain as his injured finger opened up again and blood started to spew out. Both men continued to punch and pulverize each other's body until they fell to the ground and began to wrestle. Blood was flowing from both of them. Fists and bones cracking filled the night air.

"Stop it! Stop it! Please stop it!" Tina yelped, but her pleas were ignored. She tried to call 9-1-1 and realized her battery had died. "Help me! Someone please help me! She shouted into the night with all the voice she could muster. Tina couldn't believe Mitchell's Secret Service detail was nowhere in sight. She had to do something, so she ran back to her car hoping her charger was there and she could call for help.

The men struggled to their feet and regained their footing. Worn out, hurt and broken, they took a brief time out. James wiped the blood coming from his nose with the back of his hand. He reached in his coat pocket to retrieve a tissue.

"What the hell?" He whispered as he felt a cold metal object in his pocket. The item wasn't in there when he left his home. He pulled out the shiny object. It was a gun. He didn't even own a gun.

"So James, you couldn't take a beating like a man? You had to pull out a gun. Does it make you feel like a real man? What's your next move, Congressman?"

"Shut up, Mitchell! I need to think!"

Mitchell could not contain himself as he bellowed, "What are you, mentally challenged? Did you just tell me you had to think about your next move? You really aren't a man and not deserving of my wonderful Tina's love. Give it up, James and take your pathetic weak ass home. Don't worry about the Congressional hearings in a couple of years. I'll give you a Presidential pardon. You will still be young enough to find a twenty or thirty year old who will want to settle down with your broke, disgraced behind. You can have some kids and write your memoirs. Your time of playing with the big boys is over. Now give me the gun and go home."

"You stay away from me or I swear I'll shoot."

"No, you won't. You're spineless. You don't have the guts to pull the trigger." Mitchell proclaimed as he approached James.

Pop! Pop! Pop! Pop! Pop!

Mitchell dropped to his knees. He looked at James in total disbelief and grabbed his stomach as blood dispensed from his wounds. Excoriating pain consumed his body. He jerked uncontrollably and then, with a thud, he fell flat on his face.

Silas Luxapher's demonic laughter flooded the air. James looked all around as he tried to locate the source of the disturbing noise. Out of the fog, Silas Luxapher materialized.

"Who are you?" James asked.

Luxapher's did not respond as he unloaded the rest of the bullets into James. Then he vanished back into the fog just as quickly as he had materialized.

Tina's alarming shrills infiltrated the night.

75

DAY FOUR:
I'M THE MOTHERFUCKING PRESIDENT

The annoying beeping of the alarm blared throughout my hotel suite. I was proud to say it was not just any suite, but the Presidential Suite. I was startled out of slumber; another night of true rest and sleep evaded me for the past days, weeks and months even. I hadn't had a complete eight hours of sleep since the thought crossed my mind. Well, it was more than a thought, actually a dream. But in August two thousand twelve, my dream became a reality. The Republican Party chose me at the Republican National Convention.

Since the nomination, sleep evaded me. I rolled over, silenced the blaring noise, and squinted at the fluorescent green numbers on the alarm clock. The numbers read four-fifteen a.m., yet it felt like I had barely closed my eyes. My body begged for ten more minutes of peace and quiet before I put on my mask and went on display like an ancient artifact. Ten more minutes before my transformation began, ten more minutes before I was poked and prodded like cattle on Rawhide, before I was transformed into the image that some Americans loved to hate and others just loved and worshipped. "Devil worshippers" was just one of the terms that the media used to describe my constituents. I, on the other hand, called them good ole-red blooded-true Americans.

I waited and listened to the silence. The moments prior to all the hustle and bustle, I treasured more than any other time of day. I laid on top of the duvet, thinking, hoping, and praying. Wishing on a motherfucking star. There had to be some trick that I could pull out the bag that would somehow, someway give me the edge that I so desperately needed to pull ahead in this race.

At approximately four-thirty a.m., the adjoining door opened and I could see the bright light and hear water from the shower heating to the right temperature, like it did every morning. I waited for the moment I knew would come.

"Mr. President, it's time to get your day started," Serenity, my assistant, stated as she walked into my room and began turning on the lights. Starting my shower and getting me up were only one percent of her job. "Am I showering with you this morning?"

I remained quiet with my eyes closed. I sensed her coming closer to my bed. "Do you want to shower alone this morning, Mr. President? *I required all of my staff to refer to me as Mr. President, you know like 'those Christian' people say, speak it into existence.*

'I want to be left the fuck alone." I said as I sat up on the side of the bed and ran my fingers through my silvery hair. "I have too much going on in my mind to have time for something as romantic as shower." I placed my head in my hands, covering my eyes, nose, and took a deep breath, exasperated and mentally drained. I didn't know what to do.

"Come here, Serenity," I commanded in a tone just above a whisper.

She remained frozen in time or at least it appeared that way to me. She didn't move. She stood and stared at me, judging me like all the rest. Wanting, taking just like all the rest. They all sought something from me. I was no longer a person. True enough I was flesh and bone like all the rest, but I was dead inside. It was as if I had no soul and that's why nothing seemed to bother me any longer.

"Serenity, did you hear what the fuck I said?" Startled, she jumped.

"Yes, sir."

"Yes, sir, what?" I demanded.

"Yes, sir, Mr. President," Serenity said above a whisper.

"Get over here and suck my dick," I commanded. "I'm stressed the fuck out. Why can't I get ahead in the polls?" I asked no one in particular. 'This shit is really starting to piss me the fuck off.'

'Serenity, why the fuck are you still standing way over there? What did I just tell you to do?' Is there anyone competent in this campaign besides myself?"

Too scared to answer, Serenity got on her knees and began crawling to the bed, slowly, seductively, head low, back arched. Hunger registered in her eyes as she slithered up my thigh.

"Act like you are about to suck some presidential dick, and you better act like you like it," I said as I grabbed her by the back of her head and pushed my erect dick to the back of her throat.

I closed my eyes and lay back on the bed, thinking as Serenity deep-throated me like the porn star she was before I made her my assistant. She was invaluable as an employee and performed every other role that I assigned to her. How many countless men and women had she set up and seduced for my greater good? Drug Lords, City Councilmen, Judges, Senators...You would be surprised at the length one would go to keep their secrets under wraps. The support I received was not totally because of my political views. Bribery, forgery, theft and murder all had their role in my campaign. So there was no way that I was going to be this close to the finish line and fall short. Losing was not an option.

I shook my head slightly and smirked. How could one person be so devoted to another? She offered me something that my wife never did...total devotion.

My wife was born and bred for the position of the First Lady. She had the perfect family lineage and was now poised to take her position in The White House. She loved my ambition and drive or was it the public eye and adoration that she loved? I think she loved what I could offer her, nothing more since she never worshipped the ground I walked on. I was beneath her, but she knew when we met in college that I was destined for greatness. I was the frog that she kissed and turned into a King, at least publically. She knew of my transgressions and numerous affairs, but didn't care. As long as it never went public and embarrassed her pristine image, she was willing to play the hand she was dealt if she ended up in The White House. My wife meant nothing to me other than being the piece that completed the presidential puzzle and the public loved her. They loved her southern proper manners, family values and her 'stand by your man' attitude. She knew her role and completed painting the perfect family picture.

79

It will all be over in three more days. Just three more days until I would have my new address, I hoped and prayed, but I was lazy. I wanted the results without any real actions, not on my part at least. I am what one would call a dictator, great at telling other people what to do. I just need the stupid American people to vote correctly.

The last three years flashed before me slowly, deliberately, like a nightmare. Lies had been told. I let my vision destroy my life, my marriage, my family and most importantly, my soul. My marriage had been ruined because of my dream, my vision to become the greatest leader of the free world. I took everyone and everything around me for granted. I felt as though if they didn't agree with my goal, they didn't serve a purpose in my life, in my campaign.

I used everyone and everything for my personal and political agenda and I have absolutely no shame. Why should I? I'm the next motherfucking President of the United States and when it's all said and done, it will have been worth me selling my soul to the devil.

There was just one thing that was preventing me from reaching my goal, and that was the current president's lead in the polls. What the fuck was going on? I had done everything that I knew to do to get ahead and destroy his character, but it wasn't working and I didn't know why. I am by far a better choice, a better candidate. I was born to be the president. Hell, I was born here; right here on American soil and his American heritage was still questionable, at best. The truth about his parentage and heritage still has not been proven. I mean anyone with a computer and common sense could fake a birth certificate. I graduated at the top of my class at Yale. Nothing about my lineage was questionable. I worked hard to get here, but I couldn't convince the American people that I was destined to be a leader. I closed my eyes and reminisced about the destructive things I've done to get to where I was this very moment. I will be your next president if it kills me, him or anyone in my way.

Serenity's head bobbed up and down, long deep strokes as her hands did semi-circles at the base of my dick, the warmth of her mouth and the thought of his demise caused my dick to squirt my hot juices of life down her throat. "Swallow it," I growled as my body stiffened. Seconds later, I felt relieved, relaxed and at peace. Serenity looked up at me with a devilish smile and gulped down my seed. I loved the kinky shit that Serenity did to me and for me. My wife never swallowed. She thought that was beneath her. *Hell, I could barely get a blow job from her perfect ass. And here was Serenity sucking my dick on command. That shit was sexy as hell.* Serenity flipped her bleached blonde hair to the back, licked her lips and then tongue-kissed the head of my dick. She slowly got off her knees and crawled on top of me.

"Do you love me?" She whispered in my ear as she pulled my hair and kissed me deeply.

"What do you think?" I questioned in return and grabbed her by the neck, squeezing. I flipped her over onto her back, thrusting my swollen dick into her, hard and deep. Closing my eyes, Jessica Smith's face popped into my mind; her cocoa brown, flawless skin and eyes as dark as the sea on a moonlit night made me smile. Her smile could melt even the coldest heart. I missed her so much, sometimes I convinced myself that I didn't love her, but I did. How can you love someone with your whole heart and be the cause of their death? I still can't answer that question, even with all the time that has passed. I was the reason for her demise and a part me died right along with her. Just like Serenity, she believed in me and my dream. She was willing and able to do any and everything to me and for me. I allowed her into my personal space and my heart, which was one of the biggest mistakes of my life. She got too close, knew too much. She was smart, too smart for her own good. She was my love, my soul mate, my equal. On the other end of the spectrum, she was my spy, my plant inside his campaign. I knew everything that went on inside and outside of his campaign. She even went so far as to plant information that should have ruined him, but she began to believe in the incumbent more than she believed in me. She loved me, but she no longer believed in me. She wanted to clear her conscious, come clean and tell of all the things that she had done. I couldn't let her destroy what I had built, no matter how much I loved her. She swore she would never implicate me and my role in her planting information that forty-four's campaign was funded by the Cortez drug cartel.

Domingo Cortez was the kingpin in the biggest drug cartel in North and South America. He was ruthless, heartless and everyone feared him. His hostile takeovers were the things that nightmares were made of. Whole families had been wiped from the face of the earth if they didn't cooperate with his wishes. Everyone knew of Cortez's existence, but no one knew him. He had always been a low-key, behind-the-scenes kind of kingpin. Now that Cortez had been thrust head first into a political investigation, he was not happy. He had not really funded forty-four's campaign and he was the last person that I wanted as an enemy. This thought caused my dick to go limp and the look on Serenity's face confirmed that she knew that I was no longer focused on her. "What's wrong, Mr. President?" She purred as she licked her lips, her hands simultaneously started to massage my limp dick. "Are you thinking about that bitch wife of yours?"

"Don't mention my wife with my dick in your hand," I hissed. "Do that thing you do with your tongue, you know the way you just run tongue around the head while stroking my dick." I propped myself up on the pillow and watched her suck and massage my dick in slow motion. I managed to push thoughts of Jessica from my mind and I envisioned my opponent in a noose, hanging from a tree. Closing my eyes, I smiled. Thoughts of forty-four's demise made my dick hard as granite. She smiled knowing that she accomplished what she had set out to do, which was to make me rock solid. I grabbed her by the hair and pulled her face up to kiss me passionately, purposely. I entered her, slowly, forcefully. My strokes were long, strong and punishing. She moaned, screamed and positioned her legs over my shoulders in one fluid motion without missing a beat.

82

"I want you to cum for me, Mr. President," she demanded as she repositioned herself and got on all fours. I grabbed a handful of her hair and yanked harder and deeper with each thrust. Cumming simultaneously, she got off her knees and grabbed me by the hand, leading me to the shower.

She disappeared as fast as I had cum down her throat. I allowed the warm water and overpriced body soap to wash away my morning sins. Refreshed and revived, I stepped out of the shower and just as I reached for my robe there was a knock on the door.

"Serenity, get that," I yelled, but got no response. I stumbled into the living room.

The knocking got louder, irritating. I wrapped the plush robe over my lean body and headed to the door.

Looking through the peephole, I saw a tall, stocky gentleman standing on the other side of the door.

"May I help you?" I asked through the door, agitated that Serenity had disappeared and I was forced to answer my own door and screen visitors. *Where the fuck was security? Was it so lax that any common fool off the street was allowed access to my hotel room at any time?*

"No, you can't help me, but I can help you if you allow me a few minutes of your time."

Taking a closer look through the peephole, I have no idea how he could possibly be able to help me. Hell, I don't think that he could make my situation any worse than it already was. As much as I hate to admit it, I didn't have a leg to stand on. I had lost every debate, but I looked really good doing it. I knew some people would vote for me based on my looks, not my politics, because some people are so damned stupid. I snickered to myself.

My six foot, two hundred and forty pound frame wasn't intimidated by him. *I could take him, if I had to.* Tightening my robe, I opened the door.

The man chuckled a bit when the door opened. We stood eye to eye. I felt a breeze that caused me to stumble back a bit. He stepped inside and adjusted a wooden box that he held under his left arm. What the hell was that? It felt like something or someone had passed through me, not that I had ever believed in the paranormal, but I know what I felt.

"You really are as stupid as you look on television, aren't you?" The light-skinned man stated as he shook his head from side to side. His physique reminded me of a professional linebacker; tall, muscular and stout. "You're running for President of the United States and you just opened the door for a complete stranger. Man, you as dumb as you sound on television and I didn't think that was possible."

He was right, that had been stupid of me. "Make it quick. Who are you and who sent you?" I asked. I hated that I had opened the door, but he said the magic words, that he could help me and my situation. I wanted to make this fast, either he could help me or he couldn't.

"Aren't you going to offer me a seat and a cup of coffee?" He said with a sly smirk, licking his lips.

"No, I'm not going to offer you anything until you tell me who you are, why you are here and above all else, who sent you?" I stated sternly with my arms folded across my broad chest while looking him up and down from head to toe. He was well-dressed, for sure. I could spot quality fabric from a mile away. A custom-fit Armani Collezioni wool-blended suit hung perfectly from his tall, muscular physique. He wore his suit almost as well as I did. The Prada triple-soled wingtips and suit could easily cost about four grand, I calculated in my head. This man was clearly no slouch; he had been afforded the finer things in life. *Maybe he was here to contribute to my campaign fund.* Suddenly I wasn't as defensive; perhaps he would be able to help me and my cause.

"I'm Silas Luxapher and believe it or not I hold the key to your future. You want to be President of the United States, right?" He asked, extending his right hand. When we shook hands, he held on a little longer than what was politically acceptable. I pulled my hand back and adjusted my robe again.

84

"Silas, you said that you could help me. Are you here to contribute to my campaign?"

"Of course not, what the hell would I look like throwing my money away in such a manner?" He smirked.

"Man, get the fuck out of my room before I kick your ass and call security."

"You couldn't if I had one hand tied behind my back. Calm your ass down and answer my question. Do you want to be the next President of the United States?"

"I am the next motherfucking President. Everyone in the world knows that. I want to be president, now that's funny."

I stumbled back for the second time, this time feeling a little dizzy.

"Are you okay? Can I get you some water? Maybe you need to have a seat." His voice showed concern as he put his box down on the coffee table and rushed to my side.

"Get your hands off me," I said waving him off. "I'm fine, just a little light-headed, that's all."

I made my way to the sofa and sat down. Silas kept talking, but all I heard was blah, blah, blah and whomp, whomp, whomp.

"Can you just shut the fuck up for a minute? I'm trying to think." I placed my head in my hands and rubbed my eyes. Something felt weird, but I couldn't put my finger on it. I lie back on the sofa and softly chuckled to myself. I sat up again, looked at the box on the table, and then back to Silas. I burst out laughing, hysterically this time.

He looked at me puzzled. "What's so funny? You need me. You don't believe it now, but you need me," he said, patting his chest.

"You," I answered. "You're the reason for my laughter. I need you. Mitch needs you, now that's funny as fuck. I don't need no damn-body. I got this far on my own and I will finish this race on my own."

Something about this man felt vaguely familiar, like we had met somewhere, maybe in a previous time in my life. I stood up again, staring at him, my mind racing, trying to figure out where I knew him from. I couldn't put my finger on it and I knew that I would not rest until I figured it out.

"I have something that you need, Mitchell. Everyone knows that there is no way in hell you can win this election unless your opposition pulls a disappearing act. You are losing the Presidential race." He paused, waiting on a response from me.

Finally, it clicked. I remembered where I knew Silas from as we said in unison. "What I have to offer you *will* change all of that."

He laughed a strong hearty laugh. "It took you long enough; you are one stupid motherfucker, Mitchell. It took your slow ass four days to figure this shit out. I have appeared at your door for the last four mornings and you are finally figuring it out." He shook his head with a look of disgust on his face. "Some call it déjà vu; I say you will continue to repeat the seven days prior to the biggest day of your life until you get it right."

85

Silas took a seat in the plush chair opposite me and stared at me, smirking. Then he looked at the wooden box. "Mitchell, how bad do you want the presidency? How bad do you want to live in the White House?"

Although I knew that my chances were slim, I would not dare let him or anyone else know that I felt that way. "I am the next motherfucking president, so address me as such."

Silas doubled over in laughter as tears streamed down his face. "What damn polls have you been looking at? You're losing in every one that I've seen. There is nothing wrong with being confident and secure, but you are a fucking idiot. There is no way in hell that you can win this election without some help. You have three days to wrap it up and convince those who haven't cast their votes to vote for you. The only way that you can win this election is if Satan himself offers his services."

I paused, defeated and deflated. Tears rolled down my face. I had tried everything and nothing worked. I thought that I had done a great job running a dirty ass election, but apparently not. If I couldn't fool him, who the hell could I fool?

I sat down and looked Silas dead in the eye. "What the fuck am I doing wrong? What am I going to do? I can't lose this race, I will not lose this race, but what the fuck can I do at this point?"

"I want your soul and I guarantee if you follow my instructions you will be the next President of the United States."

"How do you suppose you can pull that off?" I asked, considering anything at this point.

Silas stood and approached the wooden box that resembled a treasure chest. Gently, he rubbed his long fingers over it. "I present to you my bag of tricks, so to speak," he said and slid the box across the table.

Puzzled, I wanted to know more. I needed to know more.

"Are you willing to sell your soul to the devil?" He questioned in a low, husky, devilish tone.

"I don't have a soul. The devil took my soul and my heart a long time ago. "

"What are you willing to give for your future? What do you possess that is worth me giving you your every desire?" He took a key from a necklace he wore around his neck and placed it in the wooden box's lock. He unlocked and removed the lock. The lid of the box seemed to open on its own. A white light and red dust-like substance appeared. I jumped back fearing both the man and the box. I was scared and I can't remember being scared of anything or anyone since Domingo.

"What the fuck is that?" I yelled.

"That my boy is the key to your future." Silas reached inside the box and removed a manila envelope.

"This is all you need to win the election." He said as he laid the envelope on the coffee table.

"Why are you doing this for me?"

He belched out a deep, sinister laugh and I could swear that I saw pools of fire in his eyes. His eye color changed from blue to red and back to blue. *Who was Silas really?* I thought before touching the envelope. *Who exactly was I dealing with?*

"I can pay you anything you want, what's your fee?"

"Take a good look at me. Do I look like I need your money? I'm flawless with the exception of these beautiful tattoos that cover my perfectly sculptured body." He began unbuttoning his shirt to show off his multi-colored serpent tattoo that wrapped around his mid-section and delve into his pants. "You couldn't make enough money in ten of your lifetimes to pay me, don't flatter yourself."

"Then what do you want?" I asked, excited that my dreams were about to come true. I was really going to be the next motherfucking President.

"I want you. You can be my one million and one."

"Excuse me, you want what?" I questioned, confused.

"I want your virginity, I want to be the first man to enter you, fuck you. I want to make love to you, in case you're the romantic type. What's the proper term these days? Silas asked with a smirk. "I want to be the one to pop your cherry."

Shocked, confused and insulted, I stumbled backwards. He had knocked the wind out of me with mere words. I tightened my robe, thinking that the Presidential election could have possibly been within my reach, finally. Suddenly, I felt underdressed. His eyes scanned my frame from head to toe and those blue diamonds found a resting spot. My dick jumped, out of fear, I assume.

I opened my mouth to protest, but no sounds escaped my lips. I wanted to be offended, but I had to think about my future realistically. *What chance in hell did I have at winning the election without his help? What exactly did the envelope contain?*

"How do I know that the information that you have can secure the Presidency?"

"How do you know that it won't? I am a man of many talents. I don't play games or waste my time. Either you can take the envelope and give me what I want or you can try to win the election without me, your choice."

My body betrayed me as I felt my dick grow beneath my robe. I was hoping and praying that he didn't notice. His baritone voice caused the hairs in the back of my neck to stand at attention. It was like his voice had my dick hypnotized and it was reacting to only his voice. I tried to push any sexual thoughts to the farthest corner of my mind, but it wasn't working. It seemed as though the longer he stared at me, the harder my dick got.

He smirked at me and stepped closer. "I take it that you are seriously considering my proposal. I know that you are thinking about it, I can tell by the way your dick is responding to my voice." His eyes rested on the tent that was forming beneath my robe.

Is having everything that you ever wanted handed to you on a silver platter worth your virginity?

I attempted to touch the envelope and it moved on its own, out of my reach and changed colors. What was once a manila envelope was now red. "What the fuck was that?"

"No, no, no. The envelope belongs to you after I've been drained of all my juices and thoroughly satisfied."

"I don't know if I can do this," I whispered as I stared at the red envelope. I wasn't talking to him; I was trying to convince myself that same sex relations were wrong and immoral.

Silas was well aware of Mitchell's ego and pride. He chose to use his pride to get what he wanted.

"Just think how these stupid Americans will have to worship and respect you once you win. It's all within your reach, all you have to do is submit to me, give yourself to me. I already have your soul, I got that the when you ordered Jennifer's death. I want your body, your flesh to become one with me. Are you going to let something as minute as sex stand in your way?"

"I don't believe in homosexuality."

"I don't either, I believe in being satisfied. I believe in fucking every chance I get. I need sex more than food, my appetite is insatiable and I won't stop until I am inside of you, with or without your consent."

"You know my political platform; you know I am totally against same sex anything. I know there has to be something else that I can do. Once I'm in office, you will become untouchable as my ally."

"I'm already untouchable. I don't need you, I never have and I never will. You need me. I thought you were smarter than this. How in the hell did you make it this far? I am offering you everything that you ever wanted in life, all of the lies you told, all of the schemes you've run was for what? I'll tell you what it was for. It was for what I'm offering you right now and you are not willing to make a small sacrifice. Don't you want the world to grovel at your feet, to worship your every step? Don't you want them to hang onto your every word?"

"What if someone finds out? How will I be able to face the world, my wife and my kids? How people look at me matters more than my next breath. I can't risk being looked at as a hypocrite."

"Who's going to know besides you and me? I promise. I'm going to make you feel things that no woman ever could. I'm going to touch places that women don't know even exists. What do you want to do, Mitchell? You're wasting my time."

I closed my eyes and the visions of me in the Oval Office made me smile. Thoughts of me throwing the current president out of the White House and onto his ass made the decision for me.

I want it. I want the presidency more than I want my next breath and I am willing to do whatever it takes to get it.

My hands were shaking as I reached down and untied my robe, allowing it to fall open and expose my nakedness.

I looked at Silas. "You can have me, all of me, if you can deliver the White House on a silver platter."

"All you have to do is follow the directions in the envelope and the job is yours. Submit yourself to me and do as I tell you, no hesitation, no questions, only actions in response to my requests. Are we clear?"

"Crystal." *In less than an hour, I will have everything that I need to be who I was destined to be.*

He reached out to touch me and I flinched. His touch was gentle, almost soothing as he ran his hands over my abdomen and down into my pelvic area.

"Get on your knees and look at me," he said as he undressed, showing off a body of damn near perfection.

I kneeled in front of Silas; scared and nervous, knowing in my mind what was next. I tried to mentally prepare myself. Silas ran his fingers though my freshly shampooed hair while massaging my scalp and coaxing my face toward his penis.

Jazz Singleton

I watched as he stroked himself, growing. I saw the veins in his penis as he became longer and wider.

"Touch it, stroke it, taste it," he whispered to me.

Without hesitation, I obeyed his wishes with my eyes on the prize. I reached out to him, touching him, feeling him, massaging him, wanting him. I wasn't supposed to like touching him, but I did. My body wasn't supposed to betray me, but it did. I wanted to stroke him without being forced to do so.

He seductively ran his fingers over my lips, parting them and preparing me. Looking up at him, I felt embarrassed, insignificant. I felt like a servant and less of a man, but it felt right. I watched as precum oozed from his penis and he smeared it over my lips like Chapstick. As though it was the most natural thing in the world, I opened wide and accepted him, all of him. I had my dick sucked enough times to know how it's done, spit, alternating my hands, sucking and stroking, multi-tasking. Alternate and repeat. Why was my dick hard? I wasn't supposed to like it, I was supposed to do it and be done.

Silas's muffled moans turned me on even more. I wanted him, but all I could think of was my public image and how the world would perceive me. *A bi-sexual president? No, America was not ready for that.*

"Suck my dick, like you mean it. Like this is all you have ever wanted in your whole life. Suck it like this is your answer to all your hopes and dreams. "

I did as I was told, sucking him like I meant it, because I did. I felt him hardening in my hands, his body stiffened. He pulled out and came on my face, smiling.

I felt relieved, but unsatisfied. *This must be how my wife feels when I cum before she does.*

"Are you ready?" He asked as he pulled my face up so we were now eye to eye. "Touch me, feel the perfection that is Silas." Turning me around, my back was now to him. Fondling my hardness, he bent me over, massaging me, prepping me,

91

spreading my legs apart. I gasped, fearful, anticipating. *Eyes on the prize...1600 Pennsylvania Avenue.* Slowly, forcefully, he entered me.

"Uhggg," I groaned, gripping the headboard. I held on like my life depended on it. I watched my knuckles turn white. I tightened every muscle in my body as he repeatedly slapped me on my pale ass.

'Relax,' he whispered into me ear while pulling my hair.

Pleasure and pain coursed through every vein of my body. My low moans turned into screams of passion. "Ohhhh God, right there, damn that feels good." I hated that I was enjoying his every stroke.

I didn't know Silas hated my use of the word God, but then he pulled my hair so hard I was sure he had snatched a handful from my scalp. "God is not making you nut, I am," he said as he pushed me onto the bed and fucked me hard and fast like a ravaged animal

It seemed as though hours had passed since our sexcapade began. What started in the living room, progressed to the bedroom and then to the shower. I was drained sexually, mentally and emotionally, but my eyes were still on the prize. While watching Silas dress in silence, all I could think about was the envelope.

"Was that not the most amazing sex you've ever had in your life?"

Embarrassed and completely satisfied, I resigned my soul and nodded my head in agreement.

"I didn't hear you," he taunted. "You were screaming my name to the top of your lungs less than ten minutes ago. What's wrong, Mitchell, dick still got your tongue?"

I hated him for what I let him do to me. I hated him because I loved the feeling and wanted more of him. I stared at him, not blinking.

He stared back until I whispered my answer. "Yes, it was amazing."

I walked into the living room and picked up the envelope. My eyes gleamed and danced. Anticipating the contents and how they could destroy forty-four's chance at re-election, I knew that I had made the right decision.

Silas called my name before I had the opportunity to take possession of the envelope. "Mr. President, you have one hour to complete the task in the envelope."

"Task? What task?" I asked, frazzled and confused.

"Did I forget to divulge that little piece of information? *Bad, Silas*," he said and hit himself on the hand the same way a parent punishes a misbehaving child. "My apologies, since you are so against same-sex this and pro-choice that. You will be holding a press conference in one hour with reporters and supporters of both."

"Is this a fucking joke? You never said anything about a press conference, all you said was if we had sex, you would give me what I needed to win the election."

"I didn't divulge because you didn't ask. You have to start asking more questions. Your hour started at the beginning of this conversation, you're wasting time. The instructions are in the envelope. There will be a press conference in less than fifty-five minutes with or without you. The press conference will make you the next President of the United States or kill any of your futures thoughts in any political arena, ever."

"You're going to need this," he said and handed me the envelope. I watched him walk out the door.

I took a seat on the sofa, tore open the envelope and emptied the contents onto the table. It contained only one piece of paper with an address and the time. I glanced at the clock on the wall. It read ten minutes after eleven. The time on the paper said noon. I had fifty minutes to get dressed and make my way across town. *How in the hell was I supposed to accomplish this and what the hell did he mean when he said it could kill my political career? I am*

93

Mitchell Rush. I am the motherfucking President and no one had the power to kill my political career. I call all the damn shots. Nobody and I mean nobody tells me what to do. Silas had better remember that shit.

I arose and stepped into my walk-in closet, looking for the perfect suit for the press conference. I needed something that said confident but humble. After several minutes of debating, I chose a black double-breasted Dolce and Gabbana suit with a deep purple power tie. I laid my clothes across the bed and headed to the shower for the third time this morning, once again washing away my morning sins.

"Why are you showering again?" Serenity walked through the adjourning bedroom door.

"Where have you been?" I asked, needing to know if she had heard any of my exchange with Silas.

"Shopping, of course." She walked over to me and kissed me on the lips. "Thank you. You had Nordstrom's open early for little ole me? You do love me. I was surprised when a personal shopper knocked on my door this morning and said that you requested they open and I could shop until I could shop no more."

What the hell was she talking about?

"Where are you getting ready to go? We don't have any appearances until three p.m. and the jet will be ready to take off at one-thirty sharp."

"I have a press conference at noon. It was last minute, nothing for you to worry about." I assured her.

"You know that you only have five minutes to get there? Is it here in the hotel?" Her tone showed concern.

"Call my driver and have him meet me downstairs *now*." I instructed in a voice much louder than normal. Running out of the room, I made to my limo in record time.

After settling in and fixing myself a cocktail, I laid back and began to reminisce on the mornings events. *Who would have thought that I would have enjoyed sex with another man so much?* Thoughts of

Silas touching parts of my soul that no woman had yet to touch aroused me. I found myself reaching inside my pants to fondle myself. I wasn't focused on the world outside of my erection until I heard my name coming from the speakers. I straightened up and removed my hand while turning up the volume on the television.

"This just in...Presidential candidate Mitchell Rush has been caught in the sex scandal to end all sex scandals. Move over Monica Lewinsky, yours was nothing compared to what was sent to our studio this morning. Are you ready for this, America? Your presidential candidate is head and shoulders above the rest. He has been caught on video having sexual relations with multi-millionaire, Silas Luxapher. That's right; Mitchell Rush has given SuperHead a run for her money, based on the video I just saw. Mitchell was due to hold a conference at noon today. Was it to beat us to the punch and come out of the closet, so to speak? Mitchell Rush has run his campaign totally against all same-sex platforms. Is Mitchell gay? We have made several attempts to reach someone at his campaign headquarters with no response. This is Eboni Black for News 5 at noon. More on this story as it develops, back to you Taylor."

There I was on video in living color giving Silas head. My political career was now ruined, just like he said. I looked down at the slip of paper and dialed the number listed.

"I was waiting on your call."

"You ruined me!" I yelled into the phone.

"I told you I would. All you had to do was push your pride to the side and do whatever it took to get to the conference on time. You choose to lollygag and worry about your appearance like that's more important than world hunger and peace. You are selfish and choose to push your personal views onto the world, not because it's the right thing to do, but because you want to be right. And for that reason, you will never be POTUS."

95

DAY FIVE
OUT OF INSANITY COMES...

    With five days left before the election, presidential candidate, Mitchell William Rush was at his wits end. His poll numbers were down and he was facing with the final debate in two days. He paced his dining room floor back and forth, practically burning a hole in the Tabriz carpet he had received from the Saudi Prince three years ago as a gift. Prince David was a very generous man, so generous that he also encouraged his parents to give Mitch a large gift in the amount of $25 million dollars to help jump start his campaign to become the next president of the United States. In actuality, the $25 million wasn't really a gift, but more so a dowry for Mitch's only daughter, Elena.

    While pacing the carpet, he thought back on why Prince David was so eager for his parents to give Mitch such a lavish gift. Mitch remembered it like it was just yesterday. It was during the time when his parents were visiting the United

States to discuss foreign policies with the president. Whenever they came to Washington, DC, they would make time to stay at Mitch's home. Mitch knew the family since he was a child and after the death of his parents, they became even more prevalent in his life. This particular time when they were visiting, they brought their son, Prince David. When the prince first laid eyes on Elena, she was only seventeen. Her beauty made his heart flutter. She was the most beautiful woman he'd ever envisioned. Her porcelain skin tone accented by her rosy cheeks and lips, her unique greenish-hazel eyes, her silky long black wavy hair and her innocence ensnared his heart. Even though it was against his family tradition, he endlessly begged his parents for permission to court her until they finally agreed to a compromise. Elena could come once she completed high school and spend a year with them. If, at the end of that year, they were convinced it was true love, they would reconsider. This opportunity played right into Mitch's hands and it was a caveat that he managed to get $25 million out of the deal.

Elena learned of the arrangement when she turned eighteen. Tears rolled down her face as she screamed out, "Dad, please, please, I'm begging you, don't make me go."

Mitch pulled her close to his body and stared seductively into her big beautiful eyes. This was not a normal dad to daughter stare, but Mitch's greed lead him to use any scheme necessary to get what he wanted. That even included using his own flesh and blood.

When Mitch discovered his daughter's promiscuous behavior, he began capitalizing on it. In fact, his sick mind led him to believe she actually threw herself at him first. Mitch refused his temptations for a long time until one day his alter ego convinced him it would be okay to sleep with his daughter.

"Look, I need you to do this for me, baby girl. Do you know how much $25 million will help your daddy's campaign?"

Elena looked over at her mom, hoping she would say something, anything. Then she tried again. "But Daddy, why can't I just be a normal girl and go to college like all the other girls my age?"

His wife, Myra finally walked over to Mitch, sympathetically pleading her daughter's case.

"Dear please, how are you going to just release your daughter for an entire year to someone who is a total stranger?"

"Look Myra, you stay out of this...this will help to build her culturally. A year will go by before she knows it. Besides, he's no stranger; I've known his family for many years. I used to visit his parents when I was Elena's age. Plus he's in love with her and has promised me he will treat her like a queen."

He looked toward Elena and whispered, "You're already sleeping with anyone that breathes so why not up your game and sleep with a millionaire?"

Guilt engulfed her, and knowing all the things her dad had hanging over head, she laid her head on his shoulder and continued to cry, soaking his suit jacket. She continued to beg.

"No, Daddy, please don't make me go! I want to spend the summer with you."

He gently patted her on the back of her head.

"When you come back home, we will spend plenty of time together, but now you have to do this for me."

Elena placed a gentle kiss on his lips.

"Okay, Dad, I'll do anything for you."

Myra dared not say another word because she knew that other side of Mitch and it wasn't pretty. She looked at him with disgust in her eyes and left the room. She was well aware of the sick relationship between Elena and Mitch and it sickened her, but Myra didn't have enough evidence or the protection needed to confront them, however she was working on it!

After attempting every legal and illegal tactic in the book to win the 2012 presidential campaign, Mitch was still way behind in the polls. He didn't know what to do next, but what he was contemplating didn't look good for the incumbent. Anger controlled his every move. *I'm too close! I've come too far to lose to that egotistical, self-righteous jerk.* He could hear his dad's voice saying repeatedly in his head, "failure is not an option. There is no failure in my household. You must do whatever it takes to win."

As he picked up the phone to call his campaign manager, Josh, his intercom rang. He immediately slammed the phone down on the receiver and rushed toward the door. *Finally,* he thought, *he should have been here hours ago.*

"Josh, man, where the hell have you been? Come on up." He buzzed the door to let him in. He could hear the sound of his shoes as he climbed each stair. Once in view, Mitchell realized it wasn't Josh. "Who are you? I thought you were Josh."

"Mr. Rush, don't be alarmed. My name is Silas Luxapher. I'm here to put your worries to an end. I know how badly you want to win and I can guarantee you the election."

Mitchell, curious to hear more, opened the door wider.

"Then you're just the man I want to see. Come on in."

Mitch was actually pondering his next move on how to remove President 44 from the White House, especially after he discovered his affair with Myra. He was waiting for the right moment for Myra and the president to feel his wrath. He knew they both were conspiring against him, but Mitch was so arrogant and overly confident, he thought he could outthink them both and felt sure that he was always one step ahead.

It was during the time when Elena was doing her year sabbatical with Saudi Prince David. She had matured and certainly wasn't the young naïve girl the Prince assumed she would be.

When Prince David discovered Elena wasn't the innocent girl her dad made her out to be, his feelings for her changed instantly.

"Elena, I fell in love with you when I first laid eyes on you and was ready to take you as my wife, but it's against my tradition to marry an impure woman."

Elena was crushed. By this time, she had fallen madly in love with the Prince. He treated her well and she had never experienced such love and respect from a man before. This is why she felt she could tell him anything, but it didn't play well in her favor when she decided to confide in him.

"Prince David, I'm really feeling you and until now I've never thought lovemaking could be so special."

He stopped running his fingers through her hair and grabbed her by her shoulders.

"What did you just say, my precious lady?"

Elena smiled and murmured, "I said I love you, David. You're the only man who has ever made me feel special when we make love."

Prince David pushed her away, got up and walked across the room. He looked back at her, a frown forming a crease in his forehead.

"Are you telling me you were not a virgin? You and your dad have fooled me. I don't want anything else to do with you," he screamed. "You and your dad lied to me. This is an abomination and I'm sending you home tomorrow!"

Elena began to cry.

"Prince David, I love it here with you. Please don't send me home. I don't want to go back home to that monster. He beats my mother and forces me to have sex with him."

Prince David's eyes bucked.

"Your dad makes you have sex with him? Subhan Allah, are you serious?"

Elena shook her head as the tears rolled down her face, "It's true. He was the one who first stole my virginity."

Elena threw in a lie to help make her case look better.

"I would be pure if it wasn't for him. Please, please, don't make me go back."

The Prince's heart hurt for Elena. He walked over to her and held her close.

"Elena, I'm sorry you have experienced this in your life, but you know I can't go against my customs. My parents would have my head. You can stay for the entire year, but then you must go."

"I can't go back there," she screamed.

Prince David caressed Elena in his arms.

"Elena, does your mother know these things?"

Elena shook her head negatively. "No, my mother doesn't know. My dad said he would kill me if I told anyone."

The Prince hopped up, grabbed the phone and handed it to her.

"Here Elena, you must call your mother now and tell her what's been going on. She will help protect you."

Elena pushed the phone away.

"I can't. I don't want to bring harm to my mother. My dad is a dangerously sick man."

He dialed Elena's mother. "Elena, you must. Your mother will know what to do. She will look after you. I can't protect you once you go back to the states."

Elena could hear her mom answer the phone.

"Hello, Hello?"

She grabbed the phone from Prince David.

"Hello, Mother."

Elena could hear her mother's breathing increase.

"Elena, are you alright? What is it, child? Has something happened?"

Elena knew her mom could hear the sadness in her voice.

"Mom, I'm okay, well, not really..."

Elena's mom interrupted her. "Have you been hurt? Do I need to come there?"

She tried to mask the tears. "Mom, calm down, I'm fine. Prince David and his family have treated me very well. I wish I could stay."

"Well, then what is it, Elena? Please talk to me."

Elena took a deep breath. "Mom, please just listen."

It was very difficult for Elena to tell her mom what her father had been doing to her, but David held her hand and encouraged her.

"Go on, you can do this. You must tell her," he urged.

Looking at David, she shook her head in agreement. In a child-like voice, Elena began.

"Mom, it's about Dad. He has been forcing me to have sex with him since I was seventeen."

Elena could hear her mom's sharp intake of breath. She screamed.

"What! Dear God, I knew something wasn't right."

She heard her mom began to cry.

"I'm so sorry baby, I've failed you."

Now Elena was crying uncontrollably, too.

"Mom, no, it's not your fault. I know how badly Dad treats you."

"Elena, listen to me, I'm going to kill him. I promise you, he will pay for what he has done to my baby."

"You don't know the worst of it," Elena interrupted her mom. "Now that Prince David knows about Dad, he doesn't want to marry me anymore. He wants me to come home. Dad has destroyed my life and I hate him for it."

Elena's could hear her mom continuing to sob.

"I'm going to kill him for doing this to you, Elena. I swear, he's a dead man, somehow, someway."

Silas Luxapher appeared to be a burly man in his late fifties. He wore a dusty brown suit that looked ready for the garbage. In fact, Silas looked like he was ready for the garbage, too. As Mitch looked him up and down, his first thought was; how can this homeless looking man help me? Shit, looks like he needs my help.

"Look man, I have my final debate in two days. I have no time to waste. How the hell can you help me?"

Mitch didn't know why he was even entertaining this fellow, but he had a feeling, maybe it was hope that something good would come from this visit. Maybe he could pay him to kill the President?

"I know what you're thinking; what can this old homeless looking man do for me? How can he guarantee me a win, right?"

Mitch looked on in amazement and could only shake his head in agreement.

"Well, I'm going to tell you, and by the way, no, I'm not killing anyone for you. Not your wife or the President. What you decide to do to them is on you. I only have the tools that can help you win the election. If he dies, you die."

Mitch perked up with excitement that he didn't hear the last statement. "Oh, wow, man! How do you know these things? Who are you? How are you reading my thoughts?"

"Let's just say, I'm your life saver and that's all you need to know."

Mitch crossed his legs and leaned his body closer to Silas, waiting to hear what he had to say next. Silas reached down into his leather rustic vintage briefcase and pulled from it an antique box that looked like it was from another world. The antique box reminded Mitch of a jewelry box his grandmother owned. This caused an eerie feeling that sent chills through his entire body.

Mitch's Nana jewelry box had a lock and she kept the key hidden in a secret place. She opened it once in front of Mitch and inside a ballerina stood in the center. There was a mirror surrounded by velvet covering and other compartments held precious stones. She let him wind the silver handle and the old antique box would play music while the ballerina spun round and round. The music made him dance and dream about fun moments with his imaginary friends. His father's strict program didn't permit time for real friends.

Mitch vividly remembered staying with his dad's mother when he was only five years old and. Mitch called her Nana or Nana Zelda. Nana was a tall, frail woman. Her skin was pale and dry and had started to sag from aging. You could tell she was a beautiful woman in her early years, but the years had not been very kind to her.

Nana was extremely depressed because she had just lost her third husband, Papa Charles, six months ago. She felt she had been cursed with bad luck since birth. Even the people in her neighborhood were afraid of her because everything that came into her home would die. The neighbors would cross the street when they passed her house. After Charles' death, she became angry, extremely evil, and suicidal. She tried hanging herself, taking pills, cutting her wrists, but she still didn't die. His Daddy or Mommy would find her and rush her in to the hospital in time so that she always returned to her spooky looking home.

Five-year-old Mitch was standing next to her red cherry wooden dresser when his eyes landed on the jewelry box and he realized it was open. He picked it up and began to wind the silver handle on the jewelry box. The more he wound the handle, the louder the music played. He began spinning and spinning around the room. He was at his happiest. The music made him forget all about the beating he had just received from his dad. He was happy playing with his imaginary friends. They all laughed and danced to the music.

"What are you doing?" She screamed.

Nana was standing there in the doorway, dressed in her unattractive pastel housedress with her stockings pulled to her knees in a tight knot. Her cry startled Mitch and made him jump, which caused the old wooden jewelry box to fall from his hands and drop to the floor. The box hit the floor so hard one of the ballerina's legs broke off and rolled right next to his Nana's foot.

Mitch's eyes were big as saucers and his body trembled, "Nana I...ah, I was just listening to the music."

She grabbed him by his collar. "Didn't I tell you not to ever touch anything on my dresser? Now look what you've done."

She reached down and picked up the broken ballerina's leg from the floor. "It's broken."

"Nana, I'm sorry I didn't mean to break it, the music was so pretty."

She pushed him into the hallway, grabbed her belt and wacked him across the face one good time. Then she opened the basement door and pushed him down the stairs into the basement. "Now you will stay down there until you learn how to obey."

Mitch screamed, "No Nana, no, please let me out! Nanaaaaaaaaaaaaaaaaaaaa! Please! Noooooooooooooo."

The basement was pitch black and cold. Mitch cried and screamed until he fell asleep on the chilly, concrete basement floor. Five hours later, he woke up in the same spot. It was so dark he couldn't see his hand in front of him. Aside from the sound of his pounding heart beating rapidly from fear, he kept hearing other strange sounds. "Nana," he whispered. "Nana is that you?"

Mitch could feel a cold breeze surrounding him as if something or someone else was there with him. It made it very difficult for him to breathe. He pushed his small frame up against the brick wall, folded himself into the fetal position and escaped reality once again.

Those were not happy memories for Mitch because his grandmother psychologically scarred him for life. Although she died six years ago, he had horrible nightmares to this day. He would wake up before dawn while it was still pitch black outside and there she would be, standing right beside his bed, just staring at him. He would tuck his head underneath his blanket to make her go away.

Silas blew the dust from the box directly into Mitch's face, causing Mitch to feel like he was in a hypnotic state. Then he leaned in close to Mitch's face and stared directly into his eyes.

"I want you to hear me clearly, Mitch. There are things in this box that can perform, functions that are not of this world. And today is your lucky day, because I'm going to let you select one or a combination of the tools in the box. The tools you select will help you accomplish your mission of becoming the next President of the United States."

Even though Mitch was feeling strange, he could hear and understand every word Silas was saying to him.

"Well, Silas if you know anything about me, you know there is nothing I wouldn't give or do to become the next President of the United States."

"That's good to know because you may have to give up some things, because I can promise you, that if you use one of the tools in this box, you will definitely win."

Mitch's greed to become president outweighed anything he could possibly give up. He glared down into the box wondering how in the hell could the old rusted worn-out items help him accomplish anything. But he was running out of options. He had nothing to lose and the daze state that had come over him made him believe every word Silas spoke. Mitch reached down into the box and pulled a bobble-head doll out of it. He blew the dust and dirt from the face of the doll.

"Wow, it looks just like the President. I know I can use this."

Silas let out a deep laugh.

He began scrambling through the box, moving items from one side to the other. At the bottom of the box, he saw a blank check that was endorsed to him. He immediately grabbed it from the box and blew away the dust.

"Yeah, baby, a blank check just for me. A man could never have too much money."

The third and final tool he pulled from the box was a strange ancient gadget he had never seen before, but compared to the other remaining items, he thought it might be the best selection.

Silas glanced over at Mitch and the items he held and smiled as he shook his head in agreement.

"Mitch, during your next debate, you will deliver the best speech that has ever been delivered in history. I will be looking on."

A deep, dark, evil laugh came from Silas' mouth and suddenly Mitch found himself waking up in a room all alone.

"Silas, man, where are you?" *Where did he go? Was I dreaming? No way, it seemed too real.*

He hopped up from the couch and scoped the entire house, but he was alone. It couldn't have been a dream. He returned to the living room and lying there on the couch were the three items he had retrieved from the box.

He sat back down on the couch and laughed. "I knew it wasn't a dream."

As soon as Myra hung up from talking to Elena, she grabbed her phone to reach out to the President on his private line. *God, I dread doing this, but it's time he found out what's going on.* She and the President have been friends since they were teenagers.

Myra grew up in a political household as well, and had been surrounded by politics all her life. Her dad was the Republican governor of Washington, DC for many years. This was how she met Mitch.

"It's Myra. I need to talk to you today. Where can we meet privately?"

Myra could only hear silence on the phone. "Hold on a second," he responded.

She could hear him walking into another room.

"Okay Myra, what's going on? Are you okay?"

She cleared her throat and blurted it out. "Mitch has been having sex with Elena. She just told me everything."

Myra heard him gasped.

"What? That sick fuck! Myra, you need to take Elena and go."

She started crying again.

108

"You know I can't leave him, especially with him campaigning to take your place and become the next president. He would track both of us down and kill us. I believe he knows. He must know and now he's getting his revenge."

Myra could tell from the sound of his voice that he was confused. "Myra, what are you talking about? You believe he knows what?"

Myra didn't answer for what seemed to be at least a minute, but in actuality, it was mere seconds. He yelled again.

"Myra! What does Mitch know?"

Myra could hear the anger building in the President's voice.

"You must forgive me, but you have to know I didn't tell you because I wanted to protect your future. Elena is your daughter and Mitch must know. I know he's deranged, but do you think he's sick enough to sleep with his own daughter? He has to know she's not his daughter, that's why it was so easy to send her off with strangers."

Myra could only hear silence on the other end of the phone.

"Are you there?" She heard the President clear his throat and could tell he had started crying.

"Myra how could you do such a thing to me? After everything you put me through... leaving me for Mitch and NOW you want to come back at me with this? I don't believe you. Don't call me anymore with your lies!

"Please forgive me..." Myra was crying hysterically. She held her breath when she heard the phone click. Myra felt his anger. She loved him so dearly that knowing she had deprived him of a life with his daughter hurt every fiber of her being. *I need to get my daughter.*

Myra waited at the airport for her daughter to return. As her daughter walked all the double doors, Myra's tears began to fall. Her little girl was gone and Elena was all grown up. The words 'He needs to die' started swirling around her head. By the time Elena walked up to her mother, Myra was screaming the words.

"HE NEEDS TO DIE! HE NEEDS TO DIE!"

Elena grabbed her mother and rushed her in the car. "MOM! Calm down, he will die!" Elena grabbed her mother's hand and said, "Mom, don't worry. The Prince told me about a pill used in Saudi Arabia on people who commit heinous crimes. It's illegal here in the United States."

Myra glared over at Elena, "Well, how does this pill work?"

Elena looked out the window to explain.

"We need to put the pill in his coffee. Due to its strong taste, it won't be detected."

Myra looked her directly in the eyes. "Will this pill kill him? Will it?"

She looked back at her mother, "Mom, calm down, and to answer your question, yes, this pill will kill him in a horrific way."

"How? How horrible will it be for him?"

"About an hour after he digests the pill, it will attack his internal organs, like acid. It will start on the inside and work its way out. It is extremely painful and I promise you, he will suffer. Once it's done doing its damage his body will be filled with open sores." She hugged her mother tightly. "And get this; there's no way to detect the pill at autopsy. He showed me some pictures of what this pill does to the body. Mom, we don't need to be around when this happens. We will need leave the house or make sure he has to leave. We can't be together when it happens." She looked into her mother's eyes. "Are you sure you want to do this?"

Without any hesitation, Myra replied, "Yes."

110

It was now one hour before the final debate and Mitch was feeling overly confident. He had his unnamed gadget and bobble-head doll pushed deep down into his pocket and he kept his hand on it at all times. He felt tonight was going to be big for him. A few hours earlier, he was home alone thinking about his visit with Silas. Now he was sitting in a hotel room waiting to go downstairs for his final debate. Mitch's wife and daughter were in the bedroom, dressing and refreshing their makeup.

Josh, his campaign manager was in his face firing off questions and advice.

"Mitch, this is your big night. Do you have your cue cards? Have you memorized your ending speech? Can I get you anything? Are you wearing the black suit with blue and red tie or the blue suit with the red and blue tie? Once your wife and daughter join you on stage, embrace them with the passion of a loving supportive husband and father. The voters love to see that side of you."

"Josh, I know you're my number one fan and you want this win as much as I do. I need you to calm down."

"I'll try, man. Here is a clean copy of your speech. Is there anything else I can do for you?"

"Yes, just relax, Josh. I guarantee that we've got this debate in the bag."

"Well, Mitch, remember...?"

Mitch interrupted him in midstream.

"Look Josh, I know the last debates haven't gone in my favor and the polls are not looking great, but not to worry, I got this, okay?"

Josh smiled with confidence.

"I really feel like you do and it's going to be the one everyone remembers."

"Now, we're speaking the same language."

Mitch looked at Josh's pale, thin frame and realized that this man had worked himself down to nothing while fighting for his victory. Mitch knew Josh would do anything for him.

There was only one hour left before the debate and Mitch **111** sat calmly in his private room backstage going over his speech. Thinking back on how he got to this moment, he found it hard to focus.

At the young age of five, his father began conditioning him to become the president of the United States. It consisted of more than educational training; his dad reinforced each lesson by using his black razor belt on Mitch's behind. Mitch's dad called his belt "the enforcer" and he would use it to lash him repeatedly across his back. Mitch could never remember when he was able to just be a child. Every summer when he thought he could enjoy the time off from school, he found himself in some advanced program, learning different languages and politics. He had always been highly intelligent and well-spoken. Besides, if he didn't live up to his father's expectations, he would get beat. After the beatings, his mom would sooth his sores with salt water and iodine.

During the summer of 1967, right before Mitch's tenth birthday, he took his first trip abroad to Saudi Arabia. School was out for the summer and children were outside playing while Mitch was being shipped out to some foreign country to learn their customs and policies.

Mitch's big blue eyes filled with water as he glared up past his dad's protruding stomach. "Daddy, why are you sending me to a place where there are wars? I could get hurt."

Mitch's dad looked down at him over his horn-rimmed glasses.

"Son, we've talked about this on many occasions. You knew this time would come. It's all part of your training."

"Please, Daddy! Please don't make me go with this man. I want to stay here with you and Mommy," he screamed.

Deranged, Mitch's burly dad looked down at him, grabbed his black leather razor belt and, with all the power in his hand, swung it toward Mitch, striking him in the face and causing him to fall backward to the ground.

112

"Don't ever question what I do for you, you ungrateful punk. After all the sacrifices I've made for you."

He took his razor belt and hit Mitch several more times across his back and head.

"As long as you live on this earth, don't ever question what I do for you, you hear me, boy?"

The unbearable pain made it difficult for Mitch to speak, but he was too afraid not to. "Yes, Daddy, yes."

Mitch realized that the beatings would never end and started coping by escaping reality. Every time his dad would whack him with the belt, he would imagine all the things that made him happy. Playing with his imaginary friends was his escape when his dad beat him for what seemed like hours. His father always had a reason to beat him. It could be for not getting perfect grades in school, if he didn't answer political questions correctly, or if he didn't speak as fluently in the many languages he'd been taught. His dad would beat him until he got it right.

Mitch remembered the day that changed his life forever. He had been seventeen at the time and completing his senior year of high school. His parents had just returned home from speaking to his instructors about his final grades. He could hear the front door slam from his bedroom upstairs.

"Mitch," his dad screamed.

He could tell by the sound of his dad's voice that it wasn't good. He slowly made his way downstairs to the den, anticipating the worst.

"Yes, Dad?"

His father gave Mitch a look that made his knees buckle.

"Mitch, what is this? How could you get an A minus in your Political Science studies?"

"Huh?" Mitch managed to utter. *I can't believe he's bitching about me getting an A minus. An A minus! Nothing's ever good enough.*

This had infuriated his dad even more.

"Huh? What the fuck do you mean, huh? All the money I've invested in you and your education, you mean to tell me you can't find anything more intelligent to say. I tell you what, young man, if that's all you can say, you need to get the fuck out of my house. You can live on the streets with all those other uneducated, low-life motherfuckers."

"But Dad..."

"Don't you but dad me. You can speak seven different languages and huh is not one of them."

Before Mitch could get to safety, his dad grabbed a bat that was sitting in the corner of the living room and swung it across Mitch's head. Blood began to spill down his face. Dazed, Mitch fell to his knees.

His father was about to strike him again when Mitch began screaming for his life.

"No, Dad, no, please, please, stop."

113

Mitch's mom, Ellen, ran into the room and before his dad could strike him again, she grabbed the bat.

"Please Sam, that's enough. You're going to kill the boy."

"No son of mine will ever disrespect what I'm doing for him by bringing an A minus into my home. An A minus in the Rush's household is unacceptable. If he can't respect my rules and do what I say, just like I brought him into this world, I will take him out."

His parents tugged back and forth with the bat until with one strong pull, his dad caused her to lose her footing and fall into the fireplace, hitting her head on the corner of the marble frame. Sam ran to her side.

"Ellen, are you alright?"

He lifted her head and kept repeating her name.

"Ellen, Ellen."

114

He tried to give her mouth-to-mouth resuscitation, but she still didn't respond. Her blood covered his hands.

Mitch got up from the floor and watched his dad try to get his mom to react. Everything seemed like a dream. He hoped what he watched wasn't true.

His father began shaking, causing her blood to splash against the walls.

"Ellen, Ellen, God, no, no...Ellen, please wake up, baby, please wake up," he screamed as if the loudness of his voice would bring her back to life.

Mitch realized that his beloved mother, the one who always tried to protect him from his father, was now lifeless in the hands of the monster. Even though it was the first time Mitch had experienced death, he knew that the monster had taken his mom away from him. He could tell by the way her eyes were looking out into nowhere. And then he SNAPPED!

Reality escaped him once again. Mitch grabbed the bat responsible for this ugly scene, gripped it tightly with both hands, and began swinging at his dad's head, striking him, one blow after another. He imagined playing baseball with his dad's head, hitting one home run after another until the screams and moans coming from his father ceased and he finally fell over, next to his wife. Numbness encompassed Mitch's body and everything around him blackened. He fell to the floor next to his mom and dad, and all three of them lay there motionless. An hour later, Mitch returned to a conscious state to find himself covered, not only in his own blood, but in his parents' blood as well.

Even though Mitch had never stepped inside of a church, he knew his only source of comfort and salvation in this time of need was God. Mitch dropped his head into his lap and bawled uncontrollably screaming "Oh my God, nooooo. What have I done? Please, please, God, please bring my mommy and daddy back. I can take the beating. I'll do what he tells me to do. I will become the president of the United States. Just please bring my parents back to me."

That was the first and last time Mitch spoke to God because he felt God had failed him in his time of need. Out of touch with reality, he could hear his mom's voice.

115

"Baby, it's going to be alright. All the pain and scars will soon go away." Then his dad piped in.

"By any means, son, you must win. I didn't spend millions on your education for you to give up."

His alter ego kicked in.

"Man, you're going to jail and your dream of becoming president will be all over. You need to get your thoughts together and think up a plan."

"But how will I go on without my mommy?"

"Look, Mitch, your mom wanted you to win. She would not have allowed you to endure all those beatings if she didn't want you to win. Get up, man, get your head together, get a plan, and get out."

Sobbing and delusional, Mitch began to talk to himself.

"What kind of plan? How can I get out of this mess?"

"First, you need to stay calm. Take a shower to wash away the blood and clear your head."

He went upstairs, took a shower and dressed. Then it clicked. He realized he and dad had planned to visit the college he would be attending in the next two months, so he decided to go it alone. He packed all of his clothes and put them inside his brand new 1975 Plymouth Barracuda that his dad purchased for him as a graduation present.

Mitch's father was an obsessive person. He always made sure he was overstocked when it came to household supplies. Their guest house out back was like a grocery store. Everything he needed; food, clothing, soap, even gasoline were stored there. Mitch would have never thought that the very thing his dad obsessed about would be used to dispose of his body and all the other evidence. He return to the home and drenched both of his parents in gasoline.

116   Mitch had been on the road for three hours before he received a phone call about his parent.

Ring! Ring! Ring!

"Hello?"

Mitch could hear heavy breathing on the phone.

"Mitchell Rush?"

"Yes, this is Mitchell Rush. Who is this?"

"Mitchell, this is Officer Banks with the NYPD. Mitch, are your parents Sam and Ellen Rush."

"Yes, officer, they're my parents. Is everything alright with them?

The officer took a deep pause.

"Where are you now, son?"

"I'm on my way to college in DC. I left yesterday, but stayed over at a hotel last night and now I'm back on the road. What about my parents?" Mitch tried to appear concerned,

"There has been a horrible explosion at your home. Your home was burned to the ground and nothing is identifiable. Were your parents at home? Have you spoken to them today?"

"No, my parents would have been home and no, I haven't talked to them. I promised I would call them as soon as I arrived at the school." Although he had been expecting this call, Mitch started to cry.

"Mr. Rush, it might be best to come back home. There will be an investigation into the circumstances surrounding the fire and your parents' death. I know how important it was for your father to see you in college. Go on to school and register, then return home as quickly as you can."

Mitch wiped away his tears and smiled. He realized he had gotten away with murder.

Bam! Bam! Bam! The knock on the door startled Mitch and 117 brought him back to reality.

"Mitch, are you okay in there?"

"I'm fine, Josh. Please come in."

"Mr. President?"

"Now I like the sounds of that. Yes, Josh, how can I help you?"

"You have thirty minutes before your final debate. Is there anything I can do for you?"

"Son, you sure can. How about pouring us each a glass of scotch?" Mitch answered, putting his arm around Josh,

"I sure will." Josh rushed to the bar and poured the two drinks, handing one to Mitch.

Mitch raised his glass.

"Here's to four years of presidential bliss. Together we will bring change that will secure a second term."

"I'll drink to that," Josh murmured and raised his glass.

"OK, Josh you can head downstairs and when you're ready for me to come down, just give me a call." Mitch opened the door and gestured for Josh to leave.

Josh stopped and gave Mitch a firm hand shake.

"I'll see you downstairs, Mr. President."

Mitch smiled, closing the door behind Josh. He reached into his pocket and pulled out the bobble-head doll.

"Now, how in the hell can I use this thing and make it work for me tonight? I should have asked Silas how to use you."

He stood and stared at the doll.

Then it finally clicked. He jumped up from the sofa.

"I got it!" he shouted. "His speech! If I can use this doll to affect his speech, then I'll be able to deliver a more dynamic speech without any interruptions."

118

Grabbing tissues from the box on the table, Mitch began stuffing them deep into the doll's mouth. He made sure the tissues completely filled its mouth, hopeful it would prevent the President from speaking. For extra security, he grabbed a string and tied it around the doll's neck.

"If the tissue doesn't work, I'll choke the hell out of him."

Ring! Ring! Ring!

"Hello?"

"Mitch, you're up."

"Okay, Josh, I'll be right down."

"Good evening, my name is Walter Berkley and I've been selected by the Commission on Presidential Debates to be your moderator this evening. Welcome to the final 2012 ninety minute Presidential Debate. This debate is between the democratic incumbent and former Washington, DC governor Mitchell Rush, the Republican nominee. This final debate will follow a format designed by the Commission and will cover economic issues. It will consist of 15 minute segments with two minute questions. A coin toss was done earlier and our President won, so he will answer the first question."

"Mr. President, if you're reelected, how would you address the financial deficit?"

Number forty-four looked down at his notes and began to respond. He cleared his throat, once, twice, and then a third time.

Mitch looked out into the crowd and zoomed in on Silas Luxapher sitting dead center. He then looked over to his left and swore he saw the ghosts of his parents. They were staring directly at him, smiling. He became overly confident.

His attention turned back to number forty-four and he saw the President coughing and wheezing, until he fell to his knees. A gasp went through the entire audience.

Walter Berkley was in a panic.

"Oh my God, Mr. President! We need some medical attention for him right now." **119**

One of the cameramen came over to calm Walter down.

"Man, you have to hold it together and tell the viewer's something."

"What do you suggest I say?"

The cameraman placed a calming hand on his shoulder.

"Go to commercial and tell them the president is experiencing some illness."

Walter returned to his seat and tried to appear calm.

"Ladies and gentlemen and television viewers, we must go to a commercial break because the president seems to be experiencing some medical difficulties. We will return shortly with an update."

The onstage curtains were pulled while EMTs gave medical attention to the president. He continued to cough uncontrollably and couldn't manage to speak. After ten minutes of trying to discover the problem, they rushed him to the hospital.

Myra looked like she was about to explode. She tried to jump up from her seat, but Elena grabbed her hand and forced her to sit back down.

The president's wife and children rushed to his side.

Mitch stood at the podium and waited for his moment.

After what seemed like forever, but was in actuality was only about fifteen minutes, Mr. Berkley returned and addressed the crowd.

"Studio audience and television viewers, the president has been taken to the hospital. It appears his condition isn't serious, but we will be sure to provide updates as we get them. However, since this was to be the final debate, it is his wish to allow Mr. Rush the opportunity to speak. Since this is no longer a debate, we will allow Mr. Rush to speak for the remaining hour. Mr. Rush, you will be allowed to speak on any topic you choose. Ladies and gentlemen without further delay, Mr. Rush, your Republican nominee."

Mitch was feeling great.

"Thank you, Mr. Berkley and thanks to the Presidential Commission. My prayers go out to the President and his family and I'm hoping for a speedy recovery. Tonight, I will talk about three topics, the economy, equal opportunities, and education.

"First, I would like to speak on the condition that our economy is in and the financial deficit. Now we all know this is because of our constant ignorance to continue to bail out corporate America. The last eight years we have been rewarding corporate America for all of their wrongdoings and mismanagement by giving billions and billions of dollars to bail them out. As you can see, the economy hasn't gotten any better.

"If I'm elected president, I would like to bail out the hard-working people of these here United States. I know, you're asking how will he do that. Well, I'll tell you how. By providing each American family with $250,000 bail out money. Now, of course these bailout funds will come with stipulations. First, you must take these funds and payoff all of your outstanding debt; second, you must setup a repayment plan where payments are automatically deducted from your income. This certainly will stimulate the economy and open up opportunities for jobs. It will have a trickle-down effect because the banks will be paid back their loans, the real estate market and automotive industry will recover and the American people will have some relief. It's a clear win-win for everyone.

"My second topic is equal opportunity for all. I know you're saying he's a Republican and he only cares about his own. Well, I'm here to tell you that statement is false. Even though I'm a Republican, I believe in fairness. To backup what I'm saying and as proof, my first day in office, I will start by signing the Reparations Bill. African-Americans are the only race that have not been compensated for the wrongs committed against them. The signing of the bill will grant all African-American their forty acres and a mule or the monetary equivalent.

"My third and final topic is education. All citizens of the United States with the desire to further their education will be able to do so. I will provide financial assistance and low interest rate student loans to all students. Students who graduate with a 4.0 GPA or better will not be charged a dime. Their education will be paid-in-full by the government. Those students who find math, science, and technology interesting and exciting and can maintain a 3.5 GPA or better will also receive a free education.

"The next president of this generation will be someone who is open and ready for change. The next president will be someone who is fair, ethical, and not biased or prejudiced. The next president will be someone who can compete with other countries and prepare the people for growth by providing the proper tools. The next president will be a president who is technologically sound and one who is innovative.

"I am that president, the one who will lead the United States into the future. God bless you all and God bless these United States of America."

Everyone in the arena was shocked and moved by Mitchell Rush's speech. People were on their feet, clapping, screaming, and shouting. "Mitch, Mitch, Mitch."

Mitch looked out where his parents were and saw his dad excitedly jumping and clapping. His mom just smiled. Silas Luxapher was smiling and shaking his head. Mitch read his lips. "I told you."

Walter Berkley returned to the microphone.

"Ladies and gentlemen, and our television audience, thank you for tuning in today. We have just heard a historical speech that I think will cause many people to rethink their decision. We also have news about the President. He has recovered and he is doing very well. The hospital will be releasing him tomorrow. We will allow the President to speak on a televised special tomorrow evening."

That last statement made Mitch extremely angry, but he kept it to himself. After he left the hotel, he went to the hospital to see the president.

"You gave us quite a scare. Are you sure you're okay?" Mitch asked as he walked into the hospital room. The president sat up and gave Mitch a firm handshake.

"I'm fine, just overworked. I think I just needed some rest. It all caught up with me at the wrong time. I heard your speech was phenomenal. Congratulations."

Yes, motherfucker, what did you expect? Now I only have one obstacle in my way and that's you, but not for long. I promise you that. "Thanks, Mr. President. Now get some rest. And may the best man win."

Mitch walked out of the room and went to the men's room two doors down. He pulled out the bobble-head doll and wrapped the string around his neck as tight as possible. He could hear sirens going off and the nurses running toward the president's room screaming "code red." He pulled tighter and tighter until the doll's head fell off. Then he left the men's room.

"What's going on?" he asked a passing nurse.

The nurse looked at him and smiled.

122

"Mitchell Rush, your speech was exceptional tonight."

"Never mind that, what's going on with the president? I just spoke to him. Is he alright?"

"Mr. Rush, I'm not supposed to disclose this information, but I'm sure it's okay to tell you. The President is dead. The doctors tried everything and they still are, but he's gone. They can't explain what happened. He was fine earlier."

Mitch bent over as if he was pain.

"No! What happened? This is unreal. I just left him, he was fine and now you're telling me he's dead?"

"Sir, you must keep it down. I told you that in confidence. Please don't jeopardize my job."

Mitch walked out of the hospital. *Finally, the president is out of my way. Next on my list is that whore in my home.*

Mitch woke up in his home, on the sofa again. He was feeling great. Now that he had taken care of his opponent, he knew he would become the next president of the United States.

"Mitch, dear, breakfast is ready."

I hate that bitch. I think I'll take care of her tonight.

"Coming, Myra."

Myra was happier than usual, humming and full of energy.

"I made your favorites; turkey bacon, veggie omelet with cheddar cheese, homemade biscuits and fresh brewed coffee. I want you refreshed and relaxed so you can prepare for the final debate in two days."

Dumbfounded, Mitch looked over at Myra with a question written all over his face.

"What are you talking about, Myra? The debate was last night."

"Here dear, drink up. You must be overworked because your days are all off. The debate hasn't happen yet." Myra walked over and placed a cup full of steaming black coffee in front of him,

Mitch jumped up from the table and began to pace back and forth.

"Myra, don't play games with me."

Elena ran down the stairs into the kitchen. She grabbed a piece of bacon and began eating it.

"Mom, what time are we leaving?"

"Soon, dear, soon."

Mitch was still pacing and ranting about the confusion over what day it actually was.

"Dad, are you alright?"

He stormed over to Elena.

"What day is it?"

"It's Sunday, one day before your final debate. Dad, are you sure you're okay?"

Mitch ran to the great room, grabbed the remote and turned on the television. He realized that Myra and Elena were telling the truth. The news reporters were speculating about the future final debate.

He flopped down on the couch in disbelief. Everything that happened to him in the last two days hadn't really happened. Thoughts ran though his mind; Silas Luxapher, the debate and the death of the president.

"Myra?"

Myra and Elena was standing there, suspiciously gazing at Mitch. You could tell they thought he was really losing it.

"Yes, Mitch?"

"Where's the President?"

"What do you mean where's the President?" Myra and Elena exchanged a nervous look.

"I was just wondering if he made it back to DC."

"Oh, no, I heard he was campaigning in Illinois and would return to Washington tomorrow." He could sense her relief and that made him freak out even more.

"I can't believe this is happening. What the hell have I been doing?"

"Sleeping...okay, Mitch, I know it's been stressful for you these past few days and when I saw you knocked out on the couch, I knew you needed it. I didn't have the guts to wake you. Here, honey, drink this coffee. It will help you get your head on straight." Myra got his coffee cup from the table and walked it over to him.

Mitch grabbed the cup of coffee from Myra and took a long sip.

125

"Hmm, this is great. You're right, dear. I need to just sit here and think. So you two are going out?"

"Yes, we have some errands to run. We should be home in a few hours."

Elena walked over to Mitch and gently kissed him on the cheek.

"Bye, Dad."

DAY SIX
YOU CAN'T BEAT THE SYSTEM

"Tomorrow you promise yourself will be different, yet tomorrow is too often a repetition of today." — James T. McKay

Monday morning, the day before the Presidential election, Mitchell Rush woke at five a.m. and laid in bed staring at the ceiling, wondering how the hell he got to this place in his life. The last six days seemed like a blur, but the one thing he remembered most is that he hasn't managed to seal the deal on winning the Presidency.

Looking around the room, he absorbed how his stately condo on Fourteenth Avenue provided the sanctuary he needed to process his ineffective decisions.

"You're such a damn loser, Mitch. You know that, right?" He admitted, mumbling to himself. "This shit should be simple, the American people are stupid. All they want is for someone to tell them things will be okay. That things that were fucked up before will change for the better. They want options. They want to be saved." Sighing heavily, Mitch turned on his side.

Ring Ring Ring!

The phone's urgent tone startled Mitch out of his thoughts. He wasn't sure if it was the phone that made him jump or the fact that he is on edge due to the stress of the campaign. Win or lose, this was it for Mitch, no more trying. He is going all in with this election and he will win or...

Ring Ring Ring!

The phone rang again and interrupted his thoughts, but this time there was a buzz from the night stand. His cell phone was ringing at the same time. He answered his cell without realizing the call was from a blocked ID.

"Hello."

The caller on the other end of the phone didn't personally identify who it was, but the words that were spoken made the caller's identity irrelevant, "If you want to be President, don't answer that phone."

Looking at the ringing land line and then looking again at the cell phone, Mitch was a bit apprehensive about listening to the caller; nevertheless he certainly wanted to know how this phone call was going to change his situation. "Okay, but ump, do you know who you called?"

"Of course I do, dumb ass," mockingly spat the voice, which sounded like a female caller to Mitch.

"How'd you get my number?" he asked, looking around as if there was someone else in the room.

"You need to follow my instructions and ONLY do what I tell you to. If you don't, you will lose more than the election. I'm counting on you, Mr. Rush and you will not disappoint me. No one is to know about this call. You understand?"

"Yes I do, but..." The caller silenced him.

"Shhhh, get up and get in the shower. Keep your phone handy. I have eyes on you, Mr. President. I'll be in touch." Then the phone died.

Mitchell Rush, although not easily intimidated was taken by surprise at how willing he was to accommodate this anonymous caller. Attaining a level of frustration with himself, how could he have the mitigated gall to turn over months of planning, man power and strategizing to someone who had no name, no face and, for that matter, no personality?

"Desperate times call for desperate measures. Mr. President," he scoffed.

Eyeing the clock next to the phone, it was now six a.m., time to start the last day.

128

Buzz Buzz Buzz.

The cell phone vibrated on the bathroom counter. Mitchell wanted to test whether this was a prank of some sort so he didn't answer the call. Shortly after, he received a text message:

"Pick up the damn phone. We don't have much time."

He ignored it. Then he received another message:

"You think this is a game. Well, here you go. In thirty seconds you will receive a knock on the door. Don't answer it! If you disobey my order, he will shoot you. If you do as instructed, he will receive a call from me to stand down. Watch through the peephole."

Before he finished reading the text, he heard the knock at the door. Another text message came through: "Are you watching? LOL" Mitchell, who appeared rigidly frightened, walked to the door and looked out through the peephole.

The gunman waved his shiny weapon of mass destruction and proceeded to knock again. At that time another text message came through: "Are you done playing with me?"

This time Mitch responded: "Yes, call him off."

"Fine." Two seconds later, Mitch heard a cell phone ring on the other side of his door. He instinctively grabbed his phone tighter, held his breath and looked out the peephole. The gunman returned his gaze through the peephole Mitch used to spy on him and waved good bye.

"Now answer the fucking phone." The incoming text said.

As the phone rang, Mitch became taut and then quickly recovered his emotions to answer. "Hello." It sounded as if he had been holding his breath the entire time.

"Why Mr. President, are you okay?" The caller's cynicism filled the air.

"Yes, I'm fine," he retorted. "But I have questions."

"Go ahead, Mr. President."

"Who are you? How are you able to reach me through all my security? Why do you want me to win?" Rambling all the questions made Mitch feel futile.

129

"Well...Well...Well, Mr. President, aren't you the inquisitive one this morning." After chuckling, she continued, "You can just call me The System. Once the nomination has been accepted by a candidate I have the ability to make or break them, and their race. I can get to anybody I need to, influence anything I need to and do things wherever I need them done. And the why, well Mr. President, that's easy. Because that's what I want."

"I don't understand." He shook his head in an attempt to defuse his muddled thoughts.

"I know you don't. That's the thing. Most politicians who want to be President don't have a clue what they are asking for. They believe they can do things and make a difference, but the truth is you can't do anything without The System and all its branches."

"That doesn't sound right," Mitch quizzed.

"Really, you don't think so, huh?" Determined to prove her point, she continued. "Okay, this quack that is in office now assumes he is doing good stuff for the people. Not so, since his advisors were instructed to counsel him on the needs of the people and play on that. They want to know what the government is doing, so they instruct him to create transparency. The people want to feel their leaders care about them, so his advisors dictate to him that he needs to address how to make them feel better and be healthier. HA! These are all diversions from the real issues, but at least the people feel free, all with the permission of The System." He heard a soft giggle. "Besides, he got in because I took the day off. It seemed like the other guy was headed to the White House before he decided to pick a little rifle-toting pickle of a running mate who haphazardly started talking geography and all hell broke loose. But, trust me; a buffoon like him will never get back in office, not for the next one hundred years."

"But I thought you were the know all, be all?" He quizzed.

"No. I'm part of the 'be all' as you say. Now if you want to continue to waste the valuable time we have left finding out my who's and why's and what's, so be it!" she snapped.

"Okay wait, so what happened to you before that, when I didn't even get the nomination?" Mitch asked while becoming agitated at the thought that this person on the other end of the phone held his prior candidacy in their hands and just dropped him, but now wanted to redeem themselves.

"I told you that I handle the situation once the nominations have been determined. If you can't get your own nomination then yo ass ain't ready for the position!" she replied in an equally rebuttable tone.

"So, are you saying that...?"

Interrupting his interrogation with a lack of patience, she declared "I'm saying that the Presidents of this country are as stupid as the people they serve and the only way you are going to win this time is if I let you. That office is for a puppet and my organization is the puppet master with me at the helm. Now are you ready or not?"

"I am, but I got another question." He stopped and waited for her to indicate that he should proceed.

She responded with unmistakable exasperation. "What is it?"

"Why now? What happened to you helping me before today?"

"All that will be made clear after the election. Are you done?" He heard her slowly exhale.

Mitch could tell that his Q&A session was starting to push this puppet master of The System person over the top. "Yea, how long will I have to listen to you?" He sheepishly relinquished his will to this System.

"That's a better tone; at the rate you were going I was about to get angry. And you won't like it if I get angry. Now, we have less than twenty-four hours to work. You will listen to me until I tell you not to. On Wednesday morning, after all the numbers have been tallied and are official, you will be turned over to another division."

"And who is that?"

"That depends. Are you a praying man, Mr. Rush?" There was a teasing note in her tone.

"No, me and God have an understanding that we don't understand each other. But what does that have to do with anything?" Mitch asked.

"It determines what methods we are about to take with your campaign and what team you will be on later. But since you responded no, then you will be on Silas' team. He will contact you within the next thirty minutes. I suggest you get prepared."

"What the hell?" Mitch felt totally annoyed with all the secrecy.

The leader of The System laughed boastfully. "Yep, that's him." And then the phone died again.

Sifting through the wave of emotions he was feeling, Mitch was really captivated by the thought of finally winning the Presidency, so without further hesitation he continued to finish his morning prep work. Pulling out his press book from the night stand, he checked all the events and appearances he had scheduled for the day. Glancing at the clock, it was now eight a.m.

A rapid succession of knocks hit the door like boulders. Mitchell jumped from his chair and looked at the door, questioning if he should open it or jump out of the window.

"That's stupid! I'm too high off the ground to jump out the damn window," he said aloud while actually giving the hole-in-the-wall the once-over look. "I wonder if this is Silas?" he questioned as he timidly made his way to the door. He could hear the heavy breathing of the person on the other end; however he was too afraid to ask who was knocking. Taking small baby steps, Mitchell finally made his way to the door.

132

Silas leaned forward to take a listen. Earlier he heard a rustling of papers, but now it was quiet. While Mitchell gradually leaned against the door to look out the security hole, Silas closed his eyes and tuned into the sounds of the building. He immediately detected movement in Mitch's condo.

"Look ass, I don't have all day. Open the fucking door."

Mitch jumped back from the door, surprised that the man had heard him. He strained cautiously to avoid making a sound until he knew for sure that it was Silas at the other end of the door. Feeling a sense of urgency to say something, Mitch contemplated how he got himself into this situation and made a mental note to fire his security detail once this election was over.

"Umh, who...who...who is it?" He finally managed to mutter.

"If you don't open this door, I'm gonna to break it. And if I break it, I'm gonna to break you. Do we have an understanding?" Silas inquired.

"Silas?" Mitch asked, still unsure.

"No, the fucking tooth fairy. Now open the God-damn door!" Looking up, Silas winked at the heavens and whispered to himself, "No need calling you down here."

Mitch started to unlock the door and as soon as it was slightly ajar, Silas burst through, grabbed Mitch by his neck and held him about five inches off the floor. His swiftness during this vicious attack even amazed Mitch. Silas needed no further introduction; he had the disposition of a mobster, but much bigger and much more powerful.

"Mitchell William Rush! If you ever have me wait on you again, I will kill you. Understand?" He looked him squarely in the eyes and shook Mitch like a ragdoll. Silas saw the color start to fade from Mitchell's face and realized he couldn't utter a response because he literally had no air.

"Shit!" Annoyed at Mitchell's attempt at dying, Silas shook his head, let him go and walked over to the sofa next to the coffee table to wait for Mitch to regain his composure.

"Ughfughf, oh my God, what is wrong with you? Why the hell are you trying to kill me?"

"What did you just say to me?" Silas started to rise from the couch, already in lunging position. "Repeat that shit again and I will snap your neck and walk over your lifeless body. Let's be clear, I don't like you and don't see a need to help you, but it was a request from one of my biggest supporters so I'm helping out and doing my part for man and country." His tone sounded as if he were giving himself praise for doing this deed.

"It's God," Mitch corrected him.

"What?" Looking insulted, Silas asked, "What did you say?"

"It's God and country," Mitch repeated rubbing his neck.

"Are you a liar, Mr. Rush?" He watched Mitch's bewildered face, knowing the question seemed to come from way out of left field.

"I have lied from time to time. Why?"

"Too much rhetoric." Silas shook his head, glad that Mitch was a liar, but annoyed that he talked too much. Placing a gold box on the table, Silas advanced toward Mitchell. "Then you are a liar," he reiterated.

Mitch wasn't sure where this line of questioning was going, but the tension was beginning to heighten and he needed to be on his toes. He didn't want another episode like the one at the door just moments before to happen again. Because this time he didn't think this guy would let him live.

"Well, putting it that way, I suppose I am."

"Did you lie when asked if you were a praying man?" Raising an eyebrow, Silas looked at all the signs of weakness this man was displaying. He smelled something familiar, something he had smelled many times before and yet this time it seemed even more intoxicating than sex. Fear, fear was in the air.

134 "Ah, no," Mitch answered, shaking his head profusely. "I'm not a praying man."

"Well, okay then liar, don't use His name in my presence. If you are gonna depend on him to help you, then I can't help you." Smirking at the idea, he was convinced that Mitchell was so scared of him that he wouldn't hesitate to do anything Silas wanted him to do, even sell his soul. That thought eased Silas' temper and he began to relax on the comfortable couch. Believing that Mitch had gotten his point, he doubted that he would repeat his blasphemous statement. At least not in his presence anyway and that was all that mattered.

Silas sneered while continuing his assessment of the Presidential candidate.

"Humph, you been fucking up lately and this is your last chance. So you need me." That thought gave Silas a huge, carnal smile.

"I'm sorry..." Mitch apologized and attempted to explain what he meant.

Holding up his monstrous hand, Silas acknowledged the statement with, "Yes, indeed you are. Now close the door and sit yo ass down, so you can get these instructions."

Making a quick step to follow those simple commands; Mitch was definitely inferior to the being that was in his personal space. The sooner he did what he was told, the sooner this man would be out of his condo.

Walking briskly to the adjacent chair, he sat and waited. "Okay, I'm listening."

"Good! First things first, that call this morning was from your campaign manager telling you your schedule for the day and to confirm any changes. That schedule is null and void. The System has drafted your new itinerary along with the people you 'have' to meet by the times specified on the list." Silas slid a manila folder across the table in Mitchell's direction. He was not quick to pick it up, presuming there was more information he needed to hear before he saw the list.

"Okay, so what's first?" Mitch asked as he nodded in agreement.

"Don't interrupt me. Next, it is not for you to understand the reason behind the agenda you are to keep, you are to just do it. Your security detail has been replaced by members of The System. If you try to deviate from the schedule, notify anyone of The System or refuse to do anything on the schedule, you will be dealt with swiftly." Noticing Mitch was hanging on to every word, Silas sensed that he had a question to interject.

"DO NOT IN-TER-RUPT ME!" Silas gave a look of demonic nature while Mitch confirmed his agreement with this man by sitting back in his chair, staring glaringly at the gold box he placed on the table.

"In this box, you'll find all the tools you need to complete the task. Put it on the floor in the back of your car. The locator device will tell The System and I where you are at all times today. This..." he instructed, handing him a lapel pin of the American flag with an elephant hanging from the middle of the red strip. "Will track your conversations... ALL OF YOUR CONVERSATIONS," he advised, looking squarely at Mitchell.

"Your new security detail will consist of two cars. Both will trail behind you. Don't worry about folks recognizing you and trying to shoot you or anything like that because at each location there will be a System member posted. You will not know who they are, just know they are there. The System is providing you with a different vehicle, one that is equipped with direct communications to us. It is also bullet-proof since you will be driving yourself around." He paused and motioned for Mitchell to pick up the folder.

Mitch picked up the folder and scanned over the documents. "Umh, Silas, why am I meeting folks in a nightclub?"

Silas lowered his head. "Open it," he commanded, gesturing toward the mesmerizing gold box. Mitch wanted to take in the moment. Once he opens this box it would guarantee his Presidency. Although he wanted to rip the box open, he also wanted to savor it. As he reached to pull the antiquely etched, rectangular-shaped casing closer to him, he internally felt its power. His fingers brushed down the sides to feel the rustic hinges.

"Are you going to open it or fuck it?" Silas abruptly interrupted Mitch's thoughts.

"Open it, of course." Mitch looked at Silas, annoyed that he could be so punitive. Mitchell opened the box and attempted to decipher what he was seeing. Giving up, he asked, "What is this, Silas?"

"Those, Mr. Rush, are dissolvable patches. They are laced with a little this and a little that."

"This and that what?"

"A touch of Tedral, a lot of Digitalin and a little more Risperdal. Each patch contains a lethal dose of each. You will make contact with all those people on the list and offer to buy them a drink. When you get the drink, you will drop a patch in the drink and wait for it to dissolve." Knowing there was a question looming, Silas squinted his eyes at Mitch.

136

"But won't they see it?"

"All the people on that list drink red wine or dark liquor. So to answer your question, no, they won't see it."

Mitch picked up the list and scanned the names and faces. He recognized all the people on the list as being on the incumbent's communication team. He started whispering the names on the list to himself.

Silas interrupted, "Yes, it's his communication team. Without them, he wouldn't be as poetic and charming. His press secretary has set up a mandatory power lunch to go over the last minute details of the speaking engagement scheduled for tonight at seven."

"But the President usually doesn't publicly speak on the day before an election."

"I know, but his team has decided that with the untimely diminishing health of Justice Lawlack, he would make a last minute attempt to win voters by announcing a new appointment to the Supreme Court."

137

Astounded at the gumption that the President is willfully preying on the infirmed for his political gain, Mitch whispered, "Well, I'll be damned."

"And you shall be," Silas chuckled to himself.

"But Justice Lawlack isn't dead," Mitchell quizzed, ignoring Silas and his constant belittling remarks.

"No, she's not, but she had her advisor deliver her resignation this morning after her doctor said he was putting her in hospice care."

"That information hasn't hit the news."

"It won't hit until the President makes the announcement tonight. His candidate has already been vetted because this was an expected event. It just wasn't expected to happen today."

"Who's the candidate?"

"His name is Hector Stewner," Silas answered, rubbing his chin.

"What? You look like something's wrong with him. What's his story?"

"He doesn't have much of a story, besides being an openly gay Latino whose mother is an illegal immigrant and whose father is missing in action. His mother was willfully deported after a German family adopted him. At eighteen, he got his citizenship."

"Why the hell would he appoint him?"

"Because he's America's model story. The freedom to do and screw who you want. The freedom to search for a better life and then acquire it legally." Laughing out loud, Silas continued. "All that good, old American way bullshit. Can we get back to why the fuck I'm here?"

138 "Wow, I would have never appointed Stewner. That's just stupid."

"No, sir, you wouldn't do that. You would do worse." Silas countered, leaning back on the couch. "So Mitchell, what you're going to do today is see that sexy little doctor of yours and then head over to the Siroc. Sit at your usual table and wait for the opportunity to meet and greet the communication team. Do you understand?"

Mitchell looked violated when he realized Silas knew about his doctor appointment with Alexis. "How did you know about my doctor?"

Silas gave Mitchell an obvious look of annoyance and proceeded to make his way to the door. "I know more than you think," he answered, winking at him. "Remember to put the box on the floor in the back seat of the car. To turn the microphone on you need to hold it between your thumb and forefinger for three seconds. Once it's on it stays on. You know it's on because our conversation will come through your car speakers. When you are out of the car, you will be contacted by text message." Stopping at the door, Silas spun around, "You are always under surveillance, so don't fuck it up."

"I got that," Mitch stammered.

"Oh yeah, every person on the communication team needs a drink. Wear the glove that's in the box so you don't have direct contact with the patch and at the first sign of trouble..." Silas paused and looked directly into Mitchell's eyes. "Leave!"

Just as swiftly as he entered, Silas was gone. Mitchell closed and locked the door. He looked at the clock. It was now eleven a.m.

Today is going to be the best day for Dr. Alexis Davis; she thought as she anxiously awaited what she knew would finally come. Looking out her fifth floor window, Alexis continued to replay the last two years of her life in her head. The day she met Mitchell Rush was like any other day, but with security detail.

As Dr. Alexis Davis waited for her next patient, she thought back to their first meeting two years ago.

"Is he here yet?" Alexis asked her receptionist through the intercom system that was on her desk.

"No, ma'am, but his bodyguard is here and has scanned the whole floor."

Scoffing to herself, Alexis told the air, "Like he's that damn important." Chuckling, she continued her conversation with the receptionist. "Okay, we'll let me know when he arrives."

"He just walked in, Doctor." She responded.

Alexis looked at her watch and noted he was actually on time with about twenty seconds to spare. Nodding her head, she thanked her receptionist and proceeded to the door to meet her new sexually dysfunctional client.

Upon first glance at Mitchell, he seemed like a handsome man whose lofty presence flowed throughout the room before he even spoke a word. His attitude exuded confidence and presented a manly character that wasn't easily impressed. Through his dress shirt and suit coat, Alexis could see he readily hung out at the gym. He looked to be in his mid-thirties and she knew he was unwed. Medium length black tresses framed his face while his cheeks were osculated by dimples. He didn't look like the normal presidential candidate, but who's to say that's a bad thing, Alexis thought to herself.

"Come in, Mr. Rush" she instructed, extending her hand, "It's a pleasure to meet you."

"The pleasure is all mine, Dr. Davis," he answered. They shook hands while he gave Alexis the once over. He sized her up pretty quickly. Her business attire eloquently dressed down her perky thirty-six C cups, twenty-eight inch waistline and thirty-eight inch hips. She was definitely a visually stunning woman. Flattered by Mitchell's blatant admiration of her physical appearance, she figured his therapy session would be easy and fun. Closing the door, Dr. Davis got a chance to see Mitchell's back view. She was really impressed.

140

"So why are you here, Mr. Rush?" Alexis asked.

"Please, call me Mitch." He took a seat on the custom loveseat that sat adjacent to Alexis' mahogany Vigo chair.

"Alright, Mitch, what is going on?" She asked, crossing her ankles.

"Well, Dr. Davis."

"Please, call me Doctor."

Smirking, Mitch obliged. "Okay then, Doctor, I'm here because after the death of a close associate I started having problems sleeping. I believe that's what is causing some...uhm...well, you know."

"Okay, let's begin by you telling me about her. Were you intimate with this person?"

"Woman." He insisted.

"Excuse me?" Alexis said.

"Woman. My close associate is a woman and yes, we were intimate. I loved her a lot and she helped me on my campaign. Her death came as a complete surprise to me and it was devastating," he admitted somberly.

"I see. You say she worked on your campaign and yet the media didn't get wind of your relationship. I'm sure that would have been a scandal if they had. So was she a secret?"

"Yea, she was. She was an openly agnostic person. Although I didn't share her views on that, she would certainly have been a political thorn, had it come out. So we decided to keep our little endeavors discreet." Mitch sighed.

"Is that regret, I'm sensing? Meaning, could the secrecy and untimely death of the one you loved be causing unconscious stress that renders you unable to perform?" Alexis shifted in her seat to become more engaged with Mitchell.

"Could be. I was hoping you could tell me. Look Doc, I just want to be able to be intimate. During this time I'm running around throwing my hat in the Presidential ring and it gets lonely out there and obviously plenty of women are making advances, but I just need to be able to perform to relieve some of the tension of fundraisers, hand shaking and $10,000 a plate get-togethers."

"So what exactly happens?"

"Well, the last time was real simple, there was a nice, young lady from the campaign trail that made me feel, you know. Anyway, I took her back to my suite and we started to have sex. While I'm thrusting inside her, I closed my eyes and I saw Sheba with a cross radiating from her chest. As I kept going the cross got bigger and brighter until the light was unbearable to look at. I jumped off the woman and she was all freaked out because my dick went limp and I had started choking her. I don't know for how long, but it left bruises. My public relations representative had to take care of her so that it didn't get out. But I tried two more times with other women and the same thing happened." Resting back on the couch, Mitchell looked spent.

"Okay, so Sheba is the woman you were in love with?"

"Yes."

"And she appears to you when you are having sex with other women?"

"Yes."

"With a brightly colored cross that gets brighter?"

"The cross actually gets bigger and brighter. It comes out of her chest like where her heart is and comes towards me."

"But you said she was agnostic, so I'm confused." Alexis looked bewildered.

"Exactly, that's why I'm confused as well. "

"Okay, never mind that for now, how about the strangling. Do you get off on that?" Dr. Davis inquired.

"No, but Sheba did. She liked rough sex. Her body would respond rhythmically when I would start to choke her."

142

"Okay Mitchell, tell me about the dreams. What is with the dreams?"

"Well, the dreams are more like nightmares. I can never remember the whole thing, but all I can remember is that I'm having sex and it looks like Sheba is standing there telling me to do it."

"Do what?"

"Telling me to choke the woman I'm having sex with. To choke her harder and fuck her faster, so I do. It's like Sheba is cheering me on. Then all of a sudden I see that cross and the woman I'm fucking starts to scream 'GOD' and the cross becomes blinding. I start to sweat and my skin starts to burn. It gets harder to breath and then I wake up."

Just at the moment when Doctor Davis was about to dig deeper into the story and say something, the buzzer went off. "Okay, Mitchell, we will have to meet again next week for one hour instead of thirty minutes. This situation has a lot of things that need to be worked out and this is just not enough time. I currently have a full day, otherwise I would I have you stay, but

that's not fair to my other patients. I hope you understand?"
Alexis looked for confirmation.

"Yes, of course." He stood up to bid her farewell when he
noticed Alexis was scribbling something on a notepad. "Is that
something for me?"

"Yes, it is," she confirmed, handing him the folded sheet of
paper. "See my secretary outside to schedule your next
appointment. Thank you for coming in, Mr. Rush." Dr. Davis
politely extended her hand.

"The pleasure is all mine, Ms., I mean Dr. Davis." Winking
at her, Mitchell walked out of the office and scheduled his next
visit with the receptionist.

Alexis sat in her chair and twirled around as she
contemplated how she was going to treat Mitchell. Her practice
was more than just verbal sessions, for a nominal fee it also
involved outside assistance on rectifying the problems. Alexis
loved what she did and how she did it, but Mitchell Rush would
be a challenge. The first step for him is to call the number on the
paper and she can take it from there. As she sat deep in thought
she was interrupted by the intercom, "Dr. Davis?"

143

"Yes?"

"You have a call on line 1."

"Okay, thank you."

At that very moment when Alexis Davis reached for the
phone to take that call, her life belonged to someone else and for
the next two years The System would turn Mitchell Rush's
sexual dysfunction issues into a fishing expedition for her. She
would no longer provide therapy, but a progress report of his
treatment. They wanted to know what his behavior was like and
how he responded. Knowing the intricate details of his
nightmares will give them leverage for his manipulation. The
System ran a covert operation. She regretted giving him the
number, but the only solution was not to answer when he called.

But all that was two years ago and was finally reaching a point of finality. The bondage she was feeling was going to be lifted when Mitchell Rush, after his session, walked out of her office for the last time. Because of whom he was or what The System wanted him to be, he had single-handedly transformed her successful sexual dysfunction practice into a philandering politician hot spot. Unbeknownst to him, there were forces working to help him get elected into the White House and they were using Dr. Davis to get him there.

It seems that The System knew of all her illegal sexual exploits with her wealthy political clients. They had names, dates, and amounts of all the behind-the-scene philanderers she handled. If she wanted to stay out of jail, she had to indulge The System in their request to break doctor patient confidentiality.

"Dr. Davis?" The intercom blasted through her thoughts.

"Yes."

"Mr. Rush is here."

"Really?" she said, glancing at the clock. He was at least an hour early. "Okay, Sheila, send him in."

Within seconds, Mitchell Rush walked into her office for what she imagined would be the last time. His appearance suggested he was hiding from something. Dressed in a black hoodie and sunglasses, he didn't look his normal, well put together self. Mitchell seemed out of breath, like he had sprinted all the way to her office.

"Hello, Mitch. What brings you by so early? Something wrong?" she asked.

"Well, Doc, I'm perplexed, but I will be fine."

"Tell me about it."

"It seems that this election will be different. I've been in contact with some new supporters that have given me a wealth of information," he said while catching his breath.

Sitting back in her chair, Alexis couldn't help but wonder who these new supporters were and what they provided to Mitch to make him feel so confident. "Did you jog over here?"

"Yea, I did. My car is well... indisposed at this moment." Remembering the schedule he had to keep, Mitchell would have this meeting with Alexis, run back to the house, turn on the mic and get the car, just to come back to her office and discuss frivolous things with Alexis that he didn't mind The System listening to. He realized that he had to do all this in the next fifty-five minutes so he decided to talk fast.

"Okay, then tell me about these supporters."

Placing an envelope on her desk, Mitchell informed Alexis of the details of his early morning phone call. He also told her that he would return to have a meeting at his scheduled time, but it would be a ruse to fool his observers.

Bewildered, Alexis questioned, "So you are saying that The System contacted you?" she asked, glancing at the envelope. **145**

"Yea and they gave me some items to secure my position. I'm supposed to be wearing a wire, but it's not my scheduled time. That why I ran over here early, to tell you that after today I will be going to the White House and I don't think I can see you again," he replied. His excitement caused him to finish his sentence without taking a breath.

"I see." She sounded unsure of how to handle this news. "May I?" She asked, reaching for the envelope.

"Yea sure, go ahead. It's the wire and a list of people I need to see today and what time I gotta see them."

To her surprise she was at the top of the list. "Well, Mitchell, what are you supposed to do to or with these people?" She inquired, hoping her fate didn't rest in the hands of Mitchell Rush.

"Well, that my dear is a secret, but I know your name is on there. This is another reason I came over early to ask you to do me a favor to complete my task. So I'm asking you, not as a physician but as a friend; would you help me with something?"

Knowing The System is a force to be reckoned with, Alexis felt obliged to extend whatever assistance she could to stay in their good graces. Leaning forward, she asked, "Sure, what do you need?"

"I need you to go to lunch with me at Siroc in about ninety minutes. I will handle everything else. Once there, no matter what happens or what is said, I need you to smile and respond appropriately. Okay?"

"Okay, no problem, I think. So after our session we are going to Siroc for lunch?"

"Yep, that's it." Giving her the once over, he continued. "And as usual you look stunning, so don't change." Mitchell glanced at his watch, jumped out the chair, grabbed the envelope and headed to the door. "Look, I gotta go but before I forget, we can't talk in the car. You know, the whole microphone thing."

146

"Okay, I'll see you in twenty minutes." Alexis sat back and waved. *How in the hell did I get involved in such foolishness?* Closing her eyes and inhaling deeply, she knew she was all in.

Huffing and puffing through the streets of Washington, DC, Mitchell knew he only had a few minutes to get where he needed to be and do what he needed to do. As he approached his condo, he felt a little relieved.

"I've only got five minutes to get this microphone on," he whispered.

He pressed the magic number on the elevator pad and reached for his keys. *DING - Eighth Floor*, sounded the friendly voice of the elevator. Rushing to get the door open, Mitchell ran to the bedroom and changed his clothes. At exactly twelve-thirty, he was dressed and activating his microphone.

Heading to the lobby with the box under his arm, he did not show any anxiety or perception of nervousness. He actually exuded confidence. While waiting for the car to pull up next to the entrance, Mitchell had only one emotion as he stood with his shoulders back and head held high and that emotion was power.

Following all the instructions that were laid out for him, Mitch made his way through his performance with Alexis. She genuinely played the surprised invitee when Mitch asked her out to lunch. After little dramatization and exchanging of notes between them, they were headed to Siroc.

In his Mazda MX5, Mitchell Rush headed down 15th Avenue towards his favorite restaurant. He continued to think about his session with Dr. Davis and his unsuccessful pursuit of the White House. "Today is a game-changer." He declared his thought aloud.

"What did you say?" asked Alexis.

"Nothing, nothing at all." He glanced in the rear view mirror **147** and saw the two black sedans on his tail.

Pulling up to the valet at Siroc, Mitch noticed that the service attendants seem very placid for a Monday afternoon. No bother, he was going to get preferential treatment anyway because, after all, he is a Presidential candidate.

"Good afternoon, Mr. Rush," the young attendant said, retrieving the keys from Mitch.

"Lewis, how are you?" Mitch acknowledged the friendly face that greets him every time he visited the club.

"I'm good, Mr. Rush. Thanks for asking. How's the campaign, everything going well with that? You know you only have one more day. You are looking mighty calm, sir, for a man who may be the next leader of the free world." He ended the sentence with thumbs up.

"Everything is magnificent, Lewis, just magnificent." Mitch awkwardly looked for his secret security detail.

"Well, that is great. I'll be at the polls bright and early." The valet assured Mitchell of his intent to perform his civil duty.

"Please have my detail scan the car before you bring it back."

"Of course, sir. Have a wonderful lunch."

Mitch extended his arm for Alexis to take and nodded to the men in black. He walked into the restaurant for what he hoped to be the last time as a regular American citizen.

They were greeted by a beautiful young brunette. "Why hello, Mr. Rush, your usual table?"

"Yes, Amber, thank you." He watched her perky breasts bounce as she pranced off with two menus in her well-manicured hand and showed him to his usual table in the corner facing the window. She sat Alexis and Mitchell down for an afternoon of career advancement.

"Would you like the paper, Mr. Rush?" She asked while giving him one of those perfect smiles that made the corners of her mouth crease just enough to show her dimples and make her eyes twinkle. Her flirtation didn't go unnoticed and Mitch was flattered. The erotic thought of her using that pristine smile to greet the tip of his shaft sent an arousing picture of her bobbing and weaving her head under the table while he ordered lunch.

Mitch glanced over at Alexis, who seemed unmoved by the sexual advances Amber was making.

"Yes, Amber I would." He couldn't hide the cavalier smirk that went with the shameful warm feeling he was experiencing in his crotch over this woman at least twenty years his junior. He watched as she trotted off to fill his request.

"So, Mitch, what do we do now?" Alexis inquired.

Moving in closer to where she was positioned, he took her hand into his, winked and motioned for her to be quiet. "Well my dear, let's enjoy each other's company."

"Here you go, Mr. Rush. Is there anything else I can do for you before Cindy arrives?"

"Ah..." Chuckling, he looked at Alexis who had assumed the playful role of being his companion. "No, Amber, thank you for the paper though." He maintained eye contact with the young woman who seemed overly enthusiastic about accommodating him. Mitch tried to wipe the smirk off his face as he watched Amber start to walk away, looking defeated. "Ah, Amber? There is something."

"Yes, sir?"

"Can you tell Cindy to hurry? I have a busy schedule as you can imagine."

"Yes, Mr. Rush, I will. Have a great day." Nodding to Mitch and waving bye to Alexis, she stepped away from the table to seek out Cindy.

Noticing two unfamiliar male faces enter the restaurant, Mitchell wondered if they were his System spies.

Alexis felt a magnetic attraction to Mitch. She had just started to see the charming side of him; a side that she hadn't seen since he first came into her office.

Buzz Buzz Buzz.

Both Mitchell and Alexis looked at their phones. She saw the brightly illuminated screen on her phone and held it close to her face to read the text in private. "Why are you there?" it read. Alexis didn't even have to ask who the text was from. To her it was clear. Quickly responding, Alexis tried not to cause Mitchell alarm and hoped he didn't see her disposition change. She tried to cover it with intense concentration as she responded to the text.

"Everything alright?" he asked.

Looking flustered, Alexis murmured "Yea, I'm fine." She rubbed on his lapel to signal that she remembered the microphone was on.

149

He looked down and grabbed her shaking hand. As he pressed his lips against the back of her soft skin, he could see in her eyes that she was worried. Inhaling the mixture of her fragrance and natural smell, he smiled at her, nodded and said "Okay."

At that moment, both cellphones went off. Alexis read hers first since it was sitting on the table face-down. "Tell him you have to leave." Alexis looked around the restaurant and noticed a group of people entering the place. Looking over at Mitchell, she saw his eyesight was affixed to the door as well. Reaching into his pocket, Mitchell pulled out his cellphone to read his message. "It's Showtime!"

Rising from the table, Alexis told Mitchell she had to go to the restroom and would only be a minute. She asked him to order her a Crown and coke. He agreed and she left as Cindy appeared.

150

"Mr. Rush, I am so happy to see you. Would you like something to drink?" She asked, offering her pearly white smile.

"Yes, Cindy, it's great seeing you as well. I would like a Crown and coke for my companion and my usual." He smiled back. "By the way, Cindy, I will need the bartender to be on standby. I have great news and will be buying drinks."

"Wonderful, Mr. Rush, I will let him know. Would you care to give me a hint?" She inquired, giving him a wink. He assumed it was her attempt at being coy.

Buzz Buzz Buzz.

Mitch looked down at his phone, "No, Cindy, not yet."

He read the text. "What the hell are you doing?" Mitchell responded quickly so that he could put his phone away before his orchestrated plan unfolded. "I'm doing what you said, buying a round of drinks."

Mitchell reached into his inner pocket and pulled out the specialty glove and the container of transdermal patches. Eyeing all the jolly patrons that entered the club, he waited for the exact moment to introduce himself. Glancing at his watch, he wondered what was taking Alexis so long in the bathroom.

Buzz Buzz Buzz.

"Why did you bring her?"

"She is part of my plan," he responded.

"What is your plan?"

"You will see," Mitch retorted.

"I want to know now. What is the plan?"

"Silas, not now!" Mitchell felt really full of himself to speak to Silas in that manner.

"This is not Silas, and you will tell me the plan. By the way, did you know that your little date works for us?"

Stunned, Mitchell looked at the phone before dropping it on the table. He had divulged his inner-most secret to this woman in what he thought was confidence and now he knew it wasn't. Feeling the heat rise in his body, Mitchell needed that drink quickly and looked around until he saw Cindy headed his way with two glasses.

151

Placing the drinks on the table, Cindy must have noticed a shift in Mitchell's attitude because she inquired, "Are you alright, Mr. Rush?"

"I'm perfect. Thank you for the drink." He scooped up the glass and swallowed the contents in one gulp. "May I have another please?"

"Yes, sir. I'll be right back."

Sitting back from the table in disbelief, he wondered how long she had been working for the enemy. No matter, she was going to pay for her disloyalty. Mitchell reached over and retrieved a patch and dropped it in her drink. Swirling it around, he made sure it was undetectable.

He thought of all the things he had told her about his dreams and his sexual dysfunction. Today he even told her about being contacted by the System. That explained all the questions she had about how they contacted him and if he was wired all the time.

Shortly after he watched the patch dissolve, Alexis reappeared from the bathroom, looking flustered. She scurried to the table and took a long sip of her cocktail. Not realizing that Mitch was staring at her, she took another sip that finished off the contents.

Feeling powerful, he didn't know how long it would take for the drugs to take effect. He had to do this quickly.

Buzz Buzz Buzz.

Alexis' phone went off again. She glanced at it, but didn't read the message. Slowly laying the phone on the table, she said, "Mitch, I have to leave. I hope you understand."

"Not yet, I need to do something, remember?" He winked at Alexis and she nodded in agreement. "Come, let's do this." Leaving his phone behind, he swiftly grabbed Alexis' hand and guided her to the front of the restaurant. Seizing the microphone that the live band would be using later that evening, he began to speak.

"Excuse me, ladies and gentlemen. I have an announcement to make." Everyone stopped and looked in Mitchell and Alexis' direction. Cindy and Amber looked at the bartender and shrugged their shoulders.

Mitch greeted all the members of the communication team by name and began his plan. "As many of you know, I'm running for President and today is the last day for campaigning. I've done this thing a few times already, with no success." A few chuckles came from the crowd as well as a few nods from those affirming his statement. Shaking his head and looking over at Alexis, for timing purposes only, he continued to speak to the crowd, "I met a young man named Eric Crow Draven. He is a poet and he said something to me about my campaign that really stuck with me. He said, "*They said I was nothing, that I would become the product of the poverty and bruised personalities that raised me. They said I would never amount to anything. But I did the math, I added today, subtracted my failures and found out not only are they full of shit, they don't stand a chance when I believe in me."*

Again looking at Alexis, Mitchell pulled her closer and wrapped his arm around her waist, as he looked deep into her eyes. "Well, I believe in me and so does this woman. For the last two years, she has been my rock of Gibraltar and I can truly say that there will be no other person that will be as close to me as she is. She has recognized my greatness and for that she is one of the most valuable people in my life." Placing the microphone closer to the two of them, Mitchell cupped Alexis' face in his hands and looked deeper into her eyes to see if the effects of the drugs were starting to take over. "Knowing what we mean to each other, I have asked this wonderful woman to marry me and she accepted." Leaning over, he caressed her face and kissed her cheek. Applause filled the room, a few people were typing away on their phones, no doubt getting the word out to all the social media sites about his announcement. Alexis smiled and waved to the crowd, playing the blushing bride-to-be. As the accolades drifted off, Mitch spoke into the microphone. "Drinks for everyone, on me! No worries, Roy, I will come back there and help you pour." The audience erupted again with applause.

Assisting Alexis down from the limelight, they walked hand-in-hand back to their table. "What the hell was that?" Alexis mustered through clinched teeth.

"That my dear, was revenge. And there is more to come." Lightly pecking her on the lips, he stopped by the table to drop her off and headed to the bar. Surprised at how easy it was to kiss her, Mitch figured the drugs were taking effect, so he had to act fast.

"Hey Roy, let me line the glasses up for ya and you can just pour and keep pouring and take one for yourself. Okay?" At this point, he didn't know who to trust.

"Thank you sir, but I can't drink while I'm working."

"And who's gonna tell? Go ahead, have one with me." Looking sincere, Mitchell stepped up the charm.

"Yes, sir, just one," Roy conceded.

153

"Good, but only after we've served everybody else. We don't want them waiting." Mitch pulled glasses off the racks and out of boxes under the bar. Then he grabbed a handful of patches and started dropping them in the bottom of the glasses. He diverted Roy's attention. "So Roy, how long have you been bartending?"

Roy glanced away from the glass he had started pouring. "About four years, sir. Why?"

"Well, I was thinking that you could do that little trick where I line them up and you just pour in a straight line. You know, getting the glasses filled almost simultaneously. We have a lot of folks waiting," he indicated by motioning to the crowd that was forming at the other end of the bar.

Roy saw the line and agreed that the way Mitchell suggested would be faster, at least for the first round.

Mitchell looked over at Alexis and his anger over her deception started to brew. Roy had already filled most of the glasses, so he figured he would be okay to leave him and handle Alexis.

"Follow me," he instructed her, once he got to the table.

"Where?" She watched as he took off his coat.

"Just come on. Trust me, like I trust you," he countered, winking at her.

The drug must have had Alexis feeling comfortable with him because she agreed and followed Mitchell to the storage room that Roy left open when he ran out of glasses at the bar and had to go into their stock.

"What's going on? What about the..." She tapped her collarbone indicating the microphone that Mitchell just left behind on his coat.

"Shhhh," Mitchell hushed and looked back to make sure that everyone had a glass in hand, even the two unfamiliar faces. They seemed preoccupied, so he seized the opportunity to dip in the room quickly and close the door. Swirling Alexis around, he held her close. He felt his desire to ravish her grow in his loins and it seemed from her lack of resistance that she felt the same way.

"I know you like me, don't you Doctor?" he whispered in her ear and brushed her earlobe with his bottom lip.

"Yes, but you're my patient." He could feel her slowly giving in. Laying a hand in the middle of her bosom, he could feel the pulsating of her heart.

"Don't worry about that. After tonight, I won't be your patient anymore." Wanting to look into her eyes, he turned Alexis around. He needed to bond with the beautiful woman who deceived him and yet excited his manhood. Seizing her visual attention, he began to rub his hand down the middle of her back, softly kissing the exposed part of her neck. He felt her warm skin as he listened to her breathing. Although it seemed rushed, it was intoxicatingly filled with sexual undertones.

"Mitch...I really have to...." She started to speak, but Mitch interrupted her words with a passionate kiss that felt dominating in nature. Mesmerized by the kiss, she responded well to his advance by wrapping her arms around his neck and letting him gradually guide her body to a better position near a storage rack. He needed something sturdy and this particular rack was bolted to the floor.

When their lips parted ways, her body started to shudder. He rubbed both hands down the sides of her body slowly, stopping only when he could nestle his head between her legs. Mitchell softly traced his nails up the sides of her legs until he was able to catch the hem of her skirt. Alexis tilted her pelvis in the direction of the heat coming from his mouth and slowly leaned her head back and stretched out her arms. Accepting her invitation, he continued to pull up her skirt until her lace garter thong set was exposed. He took in a whiff of her vaginal scent and was pleased at how fresh it smelled.

He knew his time with her would be rushed since people would eventually start to look for them, but he wanted to savor as much of her as he could. Gathering her skirt into a knot around his fist, Mitchell shifted her thong to the side with the other hand and blew warm air on her exposed treasure chest.

Alexis moaned from the heat. Mitch's mind started to swing to a dark place; a familiar place he used to go to with Sheba. This might not be what Alexis wanted, but it was definitely what she deserved for her deception. Mitch licked his index and middle fingers and placed them ever so lightly on Alexis' clitoris. He rubbed in a circular motion and proceeded on the upward rotation. Then he split his fingers into a "V" exposing the little man in the boat.

Alexis was shaking with desire. The effect of the medicine was kicking in and she didn't know if she could control herself much longer. She reached down to stroke Mitch's head, but he moved, so Alexis placed her hands on her vulva and opened up wider. Mitchell liked how she was responding; she was making it real easy for him. With her juices flowing and her sweet smell coming from within, he opened his mouth and devoured her clit with warm, wet, suckling motions. Mitchell let her lips go and she shuddered.

156

His desire to punish her was causing his member to fight against his zipper. With his free hand, he set his soul free. At its full eight inches, Mitchell admired and massaged his engorged best friend. Alexis let out a slight humming sound and Mitch knew she was ready. He turned her around to face the storage rack and placed his organ between her butt cheeks. Holding tight to the knot in her skirt, he moved so close he could hear her breathing. He used his free hand and began to fondle her clit again. Circularly moving his forefinger and using his middle finger for long deep strokes, Alexis started to move her hips in rhythm. As her speed started to pick up, she arched her back, gripped the rack and lowered her head. Mitchell inserted his loin into the nearest hole. Alexis let out a scream.

Mitchell leaned in to whisper. "I know you work for them. You should have told me." The tightness of her ass was hypnotic. The effects of the medication were at their peak and took over Alexis' body. She started to lose control over her muscles and her weight shifted towards the floor. Mitchell felt there was no need to hold her skirt any longer, so he let go and laid her down on the floor. Instantly, he started pounding her ass in every position he could think of. The more he pounded, the madder he got. His disposition grew darker. He could see tears falling from her face, but he didn't care. He felt super human with rage. Alexis couldn't scream or resist the savage attack on her body, she was totally submissive, just the way Mitchell liked it.

Everything in his dreams had begun to surface yet again, the chants, the cross, the heat, and the burning. Sheba taunted him to do more. The cross was so blinding that Mitch closed his eyes, but he couldn't control the burning of his skin. Somehow he didn't care about that anymore. He was going to push through this pain to satisfy his resolution of punishment for her disgusting betrayal.

"I want you to bleed for the humiliation you have exposed me to. This is all your fault." His voice was heavy and bellowed from the dark abyss within his spirit. Almost seeming satanic, his words shrilled as they imploded her eardrums. Pounding into her, he grabbed her shoulders and tossed Alexis around like a rag doll. Briefly stopping to shove his organ into her mouth, he began to face-fuck her until she involuntarily puked. This made him angrier and he slapped her for it. Then he forced her mouth to open wider and sprayed his cum into it.

157

"Mr. Rush, are you in there? There is something wrong out here, people aren't feeling well. I'm trying to account for everyone. Hello? Mr. Rush?" Cindy frantically asked after banging on the door. Mitchell had proved his point with Alexis and proceeded to get up slowly, trying hard not to make any noise confirming his existence in the storage room. He grabbed a few beverage napkins and stuffed them in Alexis' mouth and then proceeded to fix his and her clothes before slightly opening the door to make sure Cindy was gone.

"Alright sweetheart, time to go...now," he said to Alexis' lifeless body. Then he picked her up and ran out of the storage room with her in his arms.

"Where's my car? I need my car! My fiancé fell out in the bathroom and I can't wake her up. BRING ME MY DAMN CAR!" Finding Cindy helping another patron, he commanded, "Cindy, collect my things and put them in the car. I have to take her to the hospital."

"Yes, sir." Cindy quickly gathered all of his belongings, a jacket, the doctor's purse and two cell phones and ran behind him, throwing it all into the back seat of the car.

Buzz buzz buzz.

"Mr. Rush, one of these phones has a message, sir."

"Fine, I'll take it from here," he shouted at her. He ran around to the other side, jumped in and sped out of sight.

Looking in his rear view mirror, he didn't see any security detail. That was odd. Then suddenly he heard: "Mitchell Rush, what the fuck happened in there? We have been trying to reach you and you haven't responded. We see you are just leaving the restaurant, where are you going?" The voice blasted over the radio.

"Well, first I had to take care of a snitch. Your snitch! You know, my private affairs are none of your concern and I don't appreciate..." His ranting was cut off.

"What the fuck do you mean, take care of? What did you do to Dr. Davis?"

"I handled her. That's all you need to know."

"Drop her off! NOW!" blasted the bass from the radio. The sound startled Mitchell so much that he lost control of the car and veered into oncoming traffic.

Being interrupted from his sexual escapades, Silas angrily answered the phone.

"WWHHAAAT?"

"We have a rogue," The System woman said.

"Fuck! Can't you send somebody else, I'm REALLY busy," he answered and looked down at his suitors for the evening taking turns licking his balls.

"No, dammit! So tell your little playthings it's time to go. You need to get there and take care of this!"

"Hold the fuck on, Missy! You must've forgotten who I am and what I'm capable of. I dedicated this day to you, so don't fuck with me. And as far as I'm concerned, I don't have a problem with his behavior. He would make a good candidate for my ever-growing group of concubines. So you fix your own shit. And, oh yea, tell me how it went." Slamming the cellphone back down on the nightstand, he resumed the position of getting pleasured and thought nothing else of the call.

Annoyed, The System was going to have to fix this problem the only way they knew how...violently.

Recovering from the near death experience, Mitchell cussed at the voices in the radio. "Stop talking to me. I told you I had a plan and the plan was to have Alexis stand up as my fiancé while I make the bogus announcement that we were getting married. That gave me a reason to have to buy drinks for everybody and they drank it. But then you told me that she worked for you. No, that shit right there won't fly," he declared, shaking his head and pounding the steering wheel as if The System could see him.

Headed to the interstate, Mitchell continued to have a one-way conversation with the voice in the speakers. "So yea, I may have fucked up! But what do you care? You only work on elections, remember? So work on this election! I did my part." Feeling empowered, but anxious that he may have just blown his chance for the race, he sat waiting to see what The System would say next.

After a couple of silent minutes, the voice from the speakers said. "Get off and take her to St. Elizabeth. Drop her off. There will be a gurney waiting. You won't have to answer any questions."

"I don't think so. Why do you care about what happens to her anyway?" He glanced over at Alexis who seemed to be sleeping peacefully in the passenger seat. He almost grew a conscience about what he did to her, but he second guessed those emotions remembering her betrayal of his trust.

"We don't, but she's innocent in all this."

"I don't believe that."

"I don't care. Drop her off NOW."

"NO!" he shouted.

"Then her blood will be on your hands." The radio went quiet and he didn't know what to expect. After driving on the interstate at maximum speed for the last ten minutes, Mitchell was trying to figure out his next move. He put his blinker on and attempted to get over in front of the semi-truck that was in the next lane. Halfway into the merge, the car just cut off.

In seconds, the semi careened into his car causing Mitchell to lose control. The impact tossed them around the expressway and Mitchell saw his life flash before his eyes. His head hit the steering wheel and then the window. He felt warmth run down his face and then everything went black. He heard people talking and screaming and then people were ripping at his clothes and pushing on his body. Somebody asked, "Is he dead?" And then there was only silence.

160

Sirens woke Mitchell up from what seemed like sleep, but he couldn't see anything. All he heard were muffled voices. Something about BP is stable and deep lacerations and hoping that the woman makes it. Mitchell remembered that he was hit by a truck and all the aches and pains of the accident started to come back to him. He moaned, but nobody responded. He tried to open his eyes, but they felt restrained. He assumed that these were measures the medics were taking due to his injuries.

He was torn between his feelings for Alexis' condition. He wasn't sure if he wanted her to make it or not, but his own health was more pressing. He started to feel drowsy again. It was best that he conserve his energy for now, so Mitchell drifted back off to sleep.

"Mister Rush, Mister Rush, can you hear me?" Reacting to the sound of his name, Mitchell slowly opened his eyes. He saw a middle aged woman in nursing scrubs standing over him. He began to speak, but his throat was sore and his voice was soft and raspy.

"Yes, Yes, I can hear you."

"That is wonderful, Mister Rush. Take it slow and have a sip of water for me." The nurse said, holding a cup with a straw.

He sipped and got clarity of his surroundings. Clearly, he could see it was daylight outside so he knew it was election morning. "How's the woman?"

"The woman, sir?" She looked puzzled.

"Yea, the woman that was in the car with me. How is she?" he asked.

"Oh, Dr. Davis. She is fine, sir and has been released."

"Good." Relieved that he avoided a vehicular homicide charge, but then he grew concerned about his fate on the attack. Looking over at the dry erase board across from his bed he saw the word Wednesday written on it along with the nurse's name, Peggy. "Uhm, Peggy, is today Wednesday?"

"Yes sir, it is. It's the day after the election."

"Really, did I win?"

"Excuse me sir, what did you say?"

"Did I win?" he repeated.

"Win what, sir?"

"The election. I was running for President, you don't recognize me?" The confusion was starting to make Mitchell feel tired again.

"Oh yes, Mister Rush, I know who you are. And I'm not sure how to tell you this so I'm just gonna come out and say it. No, you didn't win the election, sir. That was a long time ago."

"A long time ago? It was just yesterday. What are you talking about?" Mitch began to get annoyed.

161

"No, sir, it was a long time ago. You see, you have been in a coma for the last four years. The president won his second term four years ago, sir. I'm so sorry."

Mitchell cried.

162

DAY SEVEN
HAIL TO THE CHIEF - THE GANG'S ALL HERE

Toni and Shevaughn had decided to watch the election results together, so the Monday night before the election Toni took the short two hour flight from LaGuardia to be with her mother in Atlanta. They had invested time in this election with both of them doing volunteer work in their home state for the Democratic Party and hoped the fruits of their labor would mean a victory for the incumbent. Neither realized there would be uninvited guests watching with them.

Hunched in front of the TV, Shevaughn sat with her arms wrapped around her stomach as if she were in pain. Toni grabbed the remote from her and changed the channel. Almost every station had the election on, so she decided to try and help Shevaughn relax by popping a Netflix DVD into the player.

163

"Mom, it's too early to start watching the results. You're just going to make yourself sick."

"Too late, my stomach is already queasy. Early polls have Mitchell Rush ahead by a few points. Girl, this country will really be in trouble if he wins. This man wants to take us back to the Dark Ages."

"Which is where some of us belong."

Toni turned toward the stranger's voice. A handsome man in a blue pin-striped Brooks Brothers suit sat on a bar stool in the corner of her living room. Well, he would have been handsome, except for his pale, translucent skin and the bloody hole between his dead blue eyes. "He just wants to take us back to the good ole days."

"The good ole days for whom?"

Toni heard a deep bass voice ask and saw that the apparition had been joined at the bar by a striking onyx skin-toned man with turquoise eyes dressed in tight jeans and a t-shirt. He stood over six feet tall and when he turned to face the first speaker, Toni could see a portion of the back of his head was missing. Strangely, the wound looked fresh.

"Well, certainly not for senior citizens, women, gays, Latinos or Black folks. He wants to put us back in our place alright, right back on the plantation," the dark man countered.

"Mom, we have company." Her voice came out in a whisper.

"What...who?" Shevaughn turned to her daughter who seemed preoccupied with something or someone at the bar.

"I'm not sure? If I describe them, maybe you can tell me?"

"No need for all that, mon cherié. Tell your mother Jacques Diamante is here, along with Mr. Republican himself, Eric Becker. We just wanted to share this momentous occasion with someone near and dear to us. I mean, a Black man getting elected is one thing, folks could say it was a fluke, but to actually get re-elected for a second term, well, it makes me want to believe in miracles."

"He says to tell you that it's Eric Becker and Jacques Diamante."

"Good Lord! Where are they? Get away from them." Shevaughn's stomach lurched when she heard her daughter mention their names. *I haven't thought of them in years.*

They had been two of her biggest cases; serial murderers who viewed women as prey. She hated that her daughter still spoke to the dead, but she especially hated her talking to them.

"What are they saying?"

"No surprise, it's a political argument. Mr. Becker is a Republican, Jacques is not." Toni put her forefinger to her lips and shushed Shevaughn so she could hear their conversation.

"He's got a snowball's chance in Hell of winning. He didn't deliver on half his promises..." Eric declared.

165

"Only because the good ole boys wouldn't let him, yet he still managed to accomplish more than his predecessor." In a huff, Jacques turned his back on Eric.

"Look, I'll admit he's seems to be working for the common man, but that's something I've never been...common, I mean." Eric ran his fingers through his russet brown hair and it fell over his forehead, hiding the bullet hole.

"If, by that you're implying that I am, let me assure you that no one has ever referred to me as common." Jacques sat down on the adjacent bar stool, cocked his head to the right and boldly faced Eric with a look of defiance. The two alpha males squared off as if they were about to get into an altercation when they were interrupted.

"I think he'll win again. He's the sexiest president ever." They had been joined by a tiny woman. She wore a silver blouse, black miniskirt and four-inch black knee high boots. Toni saw her strange aura had a fiery glow.

"You don't vote for a President because he's sexy," Jacques declared with condescension.

"Maybe you don't, Daddy, but that's all the criteria I need." She ran his fingers across his chest before walking away.

"That's all the criteria you need? What...wait...*Daddy*?" The way she had said Daddy didn't sound flirtatious to Toni.

"Yep, your 'little bird' was my mother. I'm Dahlia, but folks call me Doll. It's nice to finally meet you." She stuck out her hand in an attempt to shake his, but he ignored the friendly gesture and left her hanging.

"You're Lark's kid?"

"And yours."

"Momma, there's a girl here who calls herself Doll. She says she's Jacques' daughter. I don't know why, but something about her is oddly familiar." Toni's forehead wrinkled in deep thought, but still couldn't quite put her finger on why this woman reminded her of someone. Then it dawned on her. *Doll looked a little like her play sister, MadySin! How was that possible?*

Oh my God, can that be true? It would definitely explain her homicidal tendencies. I need to investigate and see if there's any truth to that.

"Okay, so why would they all want to spend election night with us?" Shevaughn asked her daughter. Toni didn't have an answer, but Eric knew exactly why he was there.

"I can't speak for the rest of them, but you know I've always cherished being in your company, Von. Some old feelings never die. I swear the years have been kind to you, woman. You look good enough to eat."

"Oh, my God, I can't believe you're still lusting after that bitch!" A second woman, with attitude, floated into the room. Toni saw she was dressed in black from head to toe and resembled a cat burglar. *But what was wrong with her skin?* It appeared cracked, like a shattered windshield.

"Damn it, Terri, leave me alone. What happened to 'til death do us part', huh?"

"I'm afraid your lovely wife is here to see me," Jacques informed Eric and walked over to Terri, putting his arms around her waist. He tilted her head up and they kissed so deeply that, embarrassed, Toni was forced to look away. Although the first two men's death wounds were repulsively evident, she wondered why the two women seemed to be relatively unscathed.

"Then tell her to stay the fuck out of my business," he spat out, turning his focus back to Shevaughn.

Toni tried to see her mother through Eric's eyes, except like most kids; she had a hard time thinking of her as sexy. Sure, her mom had aged well. She'd gained a few pounds, but in all the right places. The fact that she followed a strict three day a week military workout regimen with her husband, Cliff, kept her body a tight size fourteen. And her beautiful salt and pepper hair appeared to be just as thick and healthy as when she was in her thirties, only now she wore it in loose curls that brushed the shoulders of her red, black and white lounging pajamas. *But sexy? Ewww.*

167

"I think Mr. Becker has a crush on you, Mom," Toni whispered.

"He murdered Tony, remember?" Shevaughn folded her arms in a huff, unable to hide the anger and pain the memory brought rushing back.

"Yes, Mom I know," she sighed, not hiding her exasperation. "My biological father...you've told me the story at least a hundred times. That was so long ago, it's all pretty much water under the bridge, isn't it?"

"Maybe for you, never for me, he was the love of my life, my soul mate." Shevaughn got up and rushed to the kitchen. Holding onto the counter for balance, she took a moment to get her emotions under control and returned with a large wine glass of red moscato. After a long sip, she put it on the maple end table next to the tan and navy blue overstuffed microfiber couch. Toni saw her hand tremble a little.

"Okay, but now you have Cliff, so let's not get all down in the dumps about it. Hey, I know...you wanna watch "Madea's Witness Protection" and take our minds off our guests and the election for a while? It's a done deal anyway. The polls have all closed except on the west coast. It'll be a while before they can calculate those results."

Shevaughn nodded in agreement and tried to force herself to concentrate on the movie, but she couldn't shake the eerie feeling that she held Eric's full attention. When the movie finally ended, she got up for another glass of wine, but once in the kitchen, Shevaughn changed her mind and got down a bottle of mango Absolut. She poured a shot, downed it in one swallow and quickly poured another. After gulping the second shot down, she got a highball glass out of her kitchen cabinet, added some crushed ice, two shots of vodka and made a Desert Sunrise with orange and pineapple juice, adding a splash of grenadine for color.

168

Upon her return, she saw Toni had switched to the USA channel, although her attention was still focused in the direction of the bar. Shevaughn stood for a moment and just watched her. Toni had grown into a beautiful young lady with caramel skin and matching tightly curled hair. She had the lean body of an athlete except for her derriere. That she got from her Mama. Shevaughn walked over to her and put her hand on her daughter's shoulder.

"Are they still here?" Shevaughn whispered, nodding in their direction.

"Yes, and by the way they were laughing, I think Jacques and Doll really enjoyed the movie, Eric not so much. Terri doesn't seem to be in the best of moods, she hardly cracked a smile. I think she's jealous of the attention Eric gives you.

"Oh, yeah, Bethany and the boys dropped in while you were in the kitchen. They said to tell you hello and that they have no hard feelings. They understand that you were just doing your job. Bethany says it was your calling."

"Them, too? Damn, Toni, can't you make them all leave?"

"Tell her I'm not going anywhere until I see if America fell for the okey-doke," Eric insisted, standing up from his stool. "You know, I don't understand why she's so hostile. If it weren't for us, she'd just be another cop, not the retired Captain of the Portsborough Police Department. We're her claim to fame, remember? We made her illustrious career."

"They'll leave as soon as the winner is declared."

Toni thought it best not to repeat all that Eric said. She watched him walk over and stand next to her mother.

"Then you might as well go back to the election results, so they can hurry up and get the hell out of my house." Shevaughn took a sip of her drink and placed the glass on the end table. When she drew her arm back, something brush against her. The hair on the back of her neck stood straight up. She knew it was Eric.

"Back the fuck up!" she snarled. It shocked Toni that her mother could feel his presence. She was used to it since she had been talking to dead people almost all her life. Then she remembered there was more to their connection. After all, her mother had been the one who shot him in the forehead and ended his reign of terror. She saw how upset her mom was and suddenly wished Shevaughn had followed Cliff's lead and gone to bed early.

The results went back and forth for a while, one minute Rich was winning, the next, they were almost tied. Then, the incumbent started to pull ahead and at 11:18 p.m., CNN declared number forty-four the projected winner.

Von and Toni shouted and hugged each other. The noise woke Cliff, who moseyed into the living room.

"Did he win?" Cliff asked, rubbing his eyes, looking like a sleepy little boy in his pajamas.

"Yep, they're saying he beat Rich in the popular and electoral votes," Toni answered. Jacques chuckled loudly over Eric's protests. "If I had anything to do with it, the band would be playing 'One Nation under a Groove' at his inauguration," he teased. Even Bethany cheered and then mentioned the President looked like he could have been one of her grandbabies.

"Except that meant he wouldn't have lived to be President. She would have killed him at birth," mumbled Belial, the tallest of the five boys. "Let's just say Mom didn't take too kindly to grandsons. She didn't want any baby boys. Why was that, Mother?"

"Don't you question me, boy," Bethany hissed and reached out to smack him on the back of his head. He ducked, dodging away and she missed.

Toni had read all of her mother's case files. She knew about the Peters case and the baby boys that had been buried on Bethany's property. She noticed the mention of killing and baby boys caught Doll's attention. Toni watched her scurry to position herself closer to the tall one. Then she reached down and brushed her hand lightly across his crotch, looking up at him with a disturbing smile on her face.

"Get away from him, you slut," Bethany shrieked, reacting before Belial had a chance to. She grabbed his hand and yanked him back into their family group. His brothers moved in unison and quickly surrounded Belial in an attempt to protect him from their mother and the tiny stranger.

Murder was definitely her turn-on. This observation made Toni's skin crawl and she turned her attention back to Eric and Jacques in time to hear Jacques' snap,

"Hey, man, you know what they say...once you go Black..."

THE AUTHORS
OF
DEADLY SINS

TL JAMES

TL James graduated with an MBA from LeTourneau University. While attending there, she developed a knack for reaching and getting down into the weeds to find the delicate details that were very important to her. She also cultivated an interest in biblical studies and research. Little did James know, but her love for alternate history, passion for research and interest in biblical studies would become an integral thread in her writing style, thus building her literary formula.

After many sleepless nights, James began penning her first speculative fictional book, with her newly born son tucked comfortably at her side. She developed the family drama storyline that showcases her love of research and biblical studies. She drew from other literary classics, such as Chaucer, Shakespeare and mythology, giving birth to the MPire Series.

C. HIGHSMITH-HOOKS

Highsmith-Hooks has been writing since she could hold a pencil. Her first book, *The Soul of a Black Woman: From a Whisper to a Shout* was published in 2002. The collection of poetry and short stories earned her a mention in Literary Divas: The Top 100+ Admired African-American Women in Literature, a 2006 Amber Books Publication.

After taking a few years off from writing, Cynthia's alter-ego Imani True collaborated with Dreama Skye on *Strawberries, Stilettos, and Steam*, a collection of erotic stories published by NCM Publishing in August, 2010. That same year, more of Ms. True's work was published in Delphine Publications' anthology *Between the Sheets*. Both books received 2011 African American Literary Awards.

In the meantime, Ms. True is gearing up for the 2012 release of *A Little Sumthin' Sumthin'*, her first work in the genre of crime thrillers. Several more will follow. Born on the east coast, C. Highsmith-Hooks is the proud mother of one son.

LORITA KELSEY CHILDRESS

Childress lives with her husband David, in Northern CA. She has three daughters and a granddaughter.

Lorita's first novel *The Turning Point of Lila Louise* was published in May 2010. She is a member of Sistahs on the Reading Edge book club. Lorita's work is featured in Gumbo for the Soul; The Recipe for Literacy in the Black Community and Gumbo for the Soul; Women of Honor Special Pink Edition. In June 2012, Lorita's latest work was featured in *Suspect; A Confessional Anthology*. Her poem: *Our History is Rich* was featured in the January/March 2010 edition of Kontagious Magazine.

Lorita recently finished her first children's book and is looking for a publisher. She is currently working on her second novel. Visit her on the web at www.loritawrites4u.com.

JAZZ SINGLETON

Singleton is a vibrant author who has been writing since middle school. In high school, Singleton used writing as a therapeutic release from peer pressure and her part-time job.

She loves books, but it was not enough to satisfy her passion. She longed to write something that showed her distinct writing style. It was only recently that her friends inspired her to return to her passion; a love of writing and storytelling. So when she decided to put her thoughts to paper she wanted to tell a story that was appealing to all. Singleton wanted to evoke an emotional response from her readers. Her compelling stories are inspired by life experiences and her topic provoking imagination.

Singleton's first novel *W vs. R: Emotional Tug of War* is a fictitious masterpiece that provides powerful insight into the lives, loves and struggles of her characters.

Singleton resides outside of Dallas, Texas with her two sons.

LINDA Y. WATSON

Watson is the author of the controversial debut novel, *Necessary Measures*. Linda lives in Indiana with her husband, Elliott, and their two dogs. Between them, they have five wonderful children who are all experiencing the joys of adulthood and four lovely grandchildren. She enjoys worshipping with her husband and church family. She also loves traveling, reading, writing, dancing and hanging out with her girlfriends.

Since she was a little girl, one of her passions was writing. While her siblings were outside playing, she would hide away in her bedroom where she would read and write poems and short stories. She dreamt of one day becoming a great writer. Her dreams became a distance memory when she became a young mom and wife at the age of nineteen.

But Linda realized it was never too late to realize her dreams and is now writing. She wrote and self-published her first novel in 2010 and is currently working on the sequel.

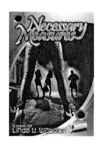

MICHELE T. DARRING

A Chicago native is finding her way in the literary industry. She is a stunning woman of sheer intelligence and is the former host of her own online radio talk show on BlogTalkRadio titled *The Daring Show*, where she was provocative and infuriating. To date, she has over 30 years of experience in using her brain and speaking her mind. She pulls no punches and is very candid and at times brash in her commentary of current events and social issues.

She prides herself on being genuine and not an expert. Her literary venture has taken off as she has established *The Daring Show Reading Club* while working to promoting authors. She is also a contributing writer for *Voices Behind the Tears*, an Anthology about Domestic Violence.

In her spare time, she has written over 15 book reviews for The Daring Show and has been featured in Writer's Vibe magazine. With numerous commentaries, she writes for her website www.thedaringshow.webs.com

She hopes to have her debut novella released in 2013.

JEAN HOLLOWAY

The daughter of an entrepreneur, Jean saw the only limitations you have are the ones you put on yourself. In the early 60s, her father owned his own cab in NY, which was unusual for a Black man armed with a tenth grade education.

Jean's debut novel *Ace of Hearts* started in 1980, in answer to a bet, yet it wasn't published until 2007. Two years later, *Black Jack* was released and *Deuces Wild* was released 10/10/10 on her 60th birthday! In November, 2011, she completed *Full House*, the 4th and final novel of her Deck of Cardz series. The moral of her story: Never give up your dream.

Jean now lives in Villa Rica, GA with her husband, Fred and their two dogs, Kayla, a Lhasa Apso and Max, an Afghan. Their six grown children all live nearby. They have ten grandchildren and three great-grandchildren.

Jean is the managing partner of her publishing house, PHE Ink - Writing Solutions Firm and an original member of the Georgia Peach Authors. You can check her out at www.deckofcardz.com.

PHE Ink is Houston's Premiere Independent Publishing House created by authors with a business mind. We bridge gaps between large publishing houses and Print On Demand companies. And our primary objective is Getting Books into Reader's Hands.

For more information, please visit www.pheinkpub.com.

CPSIA information can be obtained at www.ICGtesting.com
Printed in the USA
LVOW120103290113

317631LV00003B/149/P